About the Author

The author started writing when he had to give up politics as a choice in life and legal practice as an intellectual exercise due to a stroke which left him paralysed on the right side of his body. This book is his second publication. The author now thinks that maybe it would have been better to have become a writer than to have been a politician or a lawyer.

Ramesh Jeewoolall

THE PASSING AWAY OF A GENTLEMAN

ISBN (Paperback) 9781784559953
ISBN (Hardback) 9781786123954

www.austinmacauley.com

First Published (2015)
Austin Macauley Publishers Ltd.
25 Canada Square
Canary Wharf
London
E14 5LB

Printed and bound in Great Britain

Acknowledgments

My thanks to Yashwant and Corinne, Shyamal and Mette,
Manjula and Pooshan, Sunil, Roy Ghoorun, Prem Ramrekha
and Roshni Soopramanien.
The author would like to thank Soodesh Jooron, the New
Zealand artist who has drawn the illustration for the cover.

PART I - PREPARATION

1.THE BACKGROUND

The weather was extremely hot and the humidity content in the atmosphere was high. Everybody was suffering, the atmosphere made everybody sweat. Those who were in air conditioned offices preferred to stay indoors.

Dev was the owner and manager of a shop, called 'The Shop' in the heart of Port Louis, in Sir William Newton Street, very near to the Bank of Mauritius and the other commercial banks. He used to sell luxury articles meant for tourists and for the upper class of our society. Surprisingly, his shop was doing well, with clients from overseas as well as the locals. He could not complain that his business was not giving him satisfaction, he had three employees working for him, he treated them well and they also were satisfied with their work. One of them was his officially appointed assistant, one had the title of shop clerk and the third was the messenger and the odd-job man.

However, it looked as if Dev was not satisfied with what he was doing. His employees were dealing with the clients and looking after the accounts and purchases. He gave the impression that the shop was a burden that he was obliged to carry. But then he did not want to give up his only business. All his friends knew that Dev had bought the building that had been in a dilapidated state, he renovated and refurbished it and opened 'The Shop'.

The building that Dev had bought was standing on its own, it was a concrete building of a single story, with the shop area in the front part of the building and it had three more rooms at the rear. The biggest of the three rooms was used as a store, one of them was supposedly the canteen which was in fact used for miscellaneous duties and the third one was reserved for Dev as small office and where he used to receive his friends. In this room he had placed some sofas and easy chairs and his friends were feeling very comfortable to be in his company and the conversation used to take a lot of time of all of them.

There was no need for Dev to work for a living, he was rather well off, so was his wife and people who knew him were surprised that at his age he went into the business of opening a shop. He was getting past fifty and so many of his friends and relatives told him that it was time to start thinking for the onward journey of life, but he brushed aside all such remarks and he told them to come and have a look at what he was trying to do.

Many of his friends were skeptical that he would be able to continue with his business venture for long after having spent a considerable sum of money in setting up The Shop. The reason for this attitude was not far to seek, Dev was known for not doing the same thing for longer than a few years. He then would move on to something other, but that also not for long. So long as he does not spend his money uselessly, nobody is bothered, especially his friends who have always been his well-wishers.

Dev had been a very intelligent student and after his secondary school his father, who was a professional in the legal field, sent him to London so that he would follow his father in the same profession. The father was thinking that his son would not have any problem setting up an office. Dev could work in his Chambers and then take over when the father retired. But this was not to be. Here you have a very intelligent young man, coming from a good family, with all the tools that he would need to make a successful career, but somebody very high up decided that this was not to be. Dev threw his life's chances to the wind, or rather he was made to throw away what others crave for.

Before Dev proceeded to London for further studies, his parents wanted to get him married to a girl of their choice, who was indeed a very nice girl from an equally good family and who knew how to keep him in check on certain matters. But Dev said that he could think of marriage after his studies. In London he took on lease a flat in the area of Knightsbridge which everyone knows is a posh area and rather expensive, but who cares for money when you are young and carefree?

Dev started his studies at the University and for the first six months he was a model student, always on time for the lectures, always studying his text books and he made few friends during those days. This was a new type of behavior of Dev and his parents were confident that he has changed for the better.

But then after six months, he started getting fed up with life at the university. He met some Mauritian students and among them were some of his relatives. He became friends with them and as all of them were students, he also felt like giving his full time to studies. However, one of the group, a relative of his, was not interested in studies because he was really well off, and he became the mentor of Dev. At the end of the first year at the university, Dev passed his examinations, but after that first year, he gave up further studies for good.

He then managed to get a scholarship from the then Soviet Union. He was admitted at a university in Moscow where he again met some Mauritian students. He spent the first six months learning the Russian language at the end of which he became quite proficient. At the end of the year, he judged that the Soviet system of education aimed at students of the third world, was below his standard. He went back to England and people from the Soviet Bloc contacted him there, with the idea of recruiting him to give a helping hand to them in the World Federation of Free Trade Unions, also known as the WFTU, which was set up and controlled by the Soviet Union.

He started travelling to various countries with the officers of the WFTU. He was helping them but he was not committed to their cause. He had an independent mind and he did what he wanted to do, others could not influence him neither could they buy him or his conscience with presents of every kind. One country that he loved visiting was Guyana, then British Guiana. He met the topmost opposition leader who was then fighting for the independence of his country. Dev got emotionally involved with a sister of that political leader and both of them decided to get married. The question was where would the wedding he held? In Guyana or in Mauritius? Dev said that his parents would not appreciate him getting married but on Mauritian soil. It was accepted by the future bride and Dev told her that he would return to Mauritius and call for her after he had convinced his parents of his projected marriage.

When Dev came back, he did not have the courage to inform his parents of his plan and his parents arranged for Dev to marry another girl. This one also was very nice in manners, soft spoken and quiet. The Guyanese girl wrote several letters to Dev, but he did not reply to any of them. One day, he told a good friend of his to accompany him to the seaside where there was a high cliff and no beach. They went to the place and Dev threw in the sea all the personal effects of the Guyanese girl that he had carried to Mauritius all the way from Guyana.

Although he did not earn any academic certificate for all the time that he spent outside the country, he still gained a lot of experience that would serve him in life, but which would not be of any use when it came to looking for a job. But there was no need for Dev to look for a job because he was, and had always been, a man of leisure, we can say.

2. A CYCLONE MAY COME…

People in Mauritius were saying that we might have a cyclone in the days to come. Cyclones are a common phenomenon in Mauritius, every year there are between ten to twenty cyclones in formation in the Indian Ocean but most of them die down in the stage of formation itself. Every now and then we do experience some mild ones and people are not bothered by them and after a day or two, they go about their business as usual.

Mauritius is situated within the cyclonic belt and at times, say once in ten years, a really strong cyclone hits the country, bringing in its wake untold misery, destruction and harm. Just imagine gusts of wind blowing at more than three hundred kilometres per hour with torrential rain accompanied by flashes of lightning and peals of thunder. When the cyclone passes near Mauritius, with the eye somewhat away from the shore, the cyclone hits us only once. But when the eye of the cyclone passes over the country, we feel the effects of the wind and the rain and the lightning and thunder twice over. The danger that people experience is repeated twice for good measure.

In the eye of the cyclone an eerie calm prevails. There is no wind and no rain. It is so quiet, the leaves remaining on the trees do not tremble, and it seems that the cyclone has left the shores of the country all of a sudden. The officers from the meteorological department inform the people through the radio and television that the cyclone has not yet left our shores, in an hour or two, it will hit our country from the other side. But most persons do not pay any heed to what the officers advise. They go out just to have a look at the damage that has been caused. In an hour or two, the other end of the cyclone hits the country and this time, the damage caused is far heavier than the damage caused by the first part of the cyclone.

A cyclone is in fact a circle that is very quiet inside but which has a very disturbed atmosphere outside the circle and that the cyclonic area all around extends to a distance depending to the intensity of the cyclone. When the outer edges hit a territory, the centre remains away, the effects of only part of the cyclone are felt. When the centre passes over the territory, the effects are different, as if the people are experiencing two cyclones in an interval of a few hours, depending on the diameter of the cyclone. A period of extreme calm and then the second part of the cyclone hits and during the first part of the cyclone, the trees are shaken, the second part easily brings them down. The houses that have been damaged are blown down and those persons who did not pay much attention to the warnings have to pay dire consequences. Some persons are caught out-doors and it is not surprising that a few lose their lives.

We rarely have cyclones in the winter time and as soon as we get into the beginning of summer, quite a number of persons begin refurbishing their homes and facilities inside the houses are re-checked. It was not surprising that Dev had the installation for electricity in his shop checked, and the more so he wanted a medium sized electricity generator installed on the premises. It is well known that in a cyclone, electricity supply is interrupted or switched off, depending on the circumstances and the danger that the supply may represent. That is why people are advised to buy candles and batteries for torches and transistor radios.

Dev talked to some of his relatives and some friends about the idea of having an electricity generator installed in The Shop and everybody approved the idea. He started looking for a good electrician who could do the job to his satisfaction. He was talking to his wife Laxmi and she said

"Why don't you talk to Michael Bontemps? The person who installed the fog lights in our yard."

"I think you are right. Michael lives in the cite, a cluster of small individual houses built by the government and meant for the lower middle class, and not far from us, he is known to us and he is a good electrician," Dev replied.

"I am told that he had been to work in the Cook Islands as an electrician and he is professionally qualified as such."

"I'll go and see him tomorrow. I do not want to be caught without light if a violent cyclone would hit us this summer. We know that we have not witnessed a strong and violent cyclone for the past seven years."

The following day, Dev went to see Michael Bontemps at six o'clock in the evening because he knew that he would be home around that time. Michael was home and he was glad to see Dev. Michael's house was a concrete building, small like the hundreds of houses in the cite. It was a completely detached building with a tiny garden in front and another at the rear of the building. Dev was taken in the small sitting-cum-dining room and they talked about this and that, but mostly about politics. Both Dev and Michael were supporters of the party that had been in government for the past ten years.

Finally, Michael asked Dev "What can I do for you? You would not have come to my place had you not had something to tell me."

"I do need your services. Are you still employed as the Chief Electrician for that hotel complex at Belle Mare?"

"No, I reached retirement age about six months ago, there is no need for me to work, though I am still in good health and as strong as ever. I have now gone freelance and you would be surprised if I were to tell you that now I have more work than ever. So many persons contact me to install electricity wires and equipment in their homes, others want me to redo the wiring and still others want new equipment in their old homes. I have been thinking if I have not wasted my time by being employed by others," Michael said.

"You must recruit a few assistants as you have so much work."

"Oh no, never. I do not like to have assistants as you know. Whatever work I undertake, I start it and I complete it with my own hands. I do not want to be saddled with sloppy work that will not give satisfaction to the person who entrusts me with some job."

"This is exactly the reason for which I prefer you to do whatever electrical work I want done. Now I need you to verify the installation of the wires in a shop I have bought in Port Louis. And I also want you to install a medium-sized electricity generator to service the shop in case there is a problem with the electricity supply."

"It is a good idea, but you must not delay, for we are already in the cyclonic period."

"I would like you to come to The Shop tomorrow, have a look at what needs to be done and start work tomorrow itself if you can afford it, if you have time I mean."

"Oh no, for the three coming days I am really busy, I can't free myself. Even after that, two other persons are waiting for me, but I haven't yet given a date to them. On the fourth day from now, I shall call on you at The Shop and then we shall see what needs to be done. I cannot refuse you any service after all the help that you have extended to me in the past." so said the electrician.

Before parting, Dev indicated the location of his shop to the electrician. When he arrived home, he looked very happy, so much so that his wife Laxmi asked him the reason for his happiness. He simply said that the electrician has accepted to look at the electrical works in the shop.

3. SOME HAVE SOME MONEY, OTHERS NOT

The weather was still very hot and humid and people were saying that if there would have been some rain, the temperature might go down slightly. But there was no rain and the temperature refused to go down. People were suffering and the animals also were suffering. Dev was musing, this is a funny world in which we live. From October onwards, we are in the summer season and people start complaining of the hot weather. From April onwards, we are in the winter season and people complain of the cold weather, though it is neither very hot nor very cold in the country. If God would have created only a mild weather with a fixed temperature of say eighteen degrees centigrade, neither hot nor cold, would everybody be satisfied? But then would people be ever satisfied with what they experience? Complaining is in the genes of human beings, do what you like they will never give up their habit of complaining.

Michael the electrician came to the shop of Dev. He had a look at the electrical wiring work and the other electrical installation.

He said, "Mr Dev, I would advise you to redo the wiring, I can do it in two days. What is your opinion?"

"Your opinion is mine as well. Make a list of what you need to buy and start your work: And what about the generator?"

"You don't really need a generator in the shop according to me. Maybe in extreme cases when there is an interruption in the supply of electricity by the Central Electricity Board you would need a back-up system?"

"Yes, and I would like to have one, just in case…" was Dev's reply.

"It has to be outside the shop. Do you have the space?"

"I think so. Come with me."

At the rear of the building, there was a narrow space where the generator could be sort of housed. "I would advise you to get a construction worker to put up a structure for the generator. It should be about one metre in height and about a meter and a half in length and it would be advisable to have a concrete cover."

"Where can I get somebody to do the job? I'll need a mason for that job isn't it?" Dev asked.

"If you ask me to get somebody for the job, I can ask one of my cousins who works in the construction sector if he can do it."

"Please do, and convince him to come tomorrow. That will help me," said Dev.

Dev gave some money to Michael to buy the electrical wires and other accessories and asked him to have a look at the type of generator that would be suitable for The Shop.

Michael came back in about two hours with the electric wires and the accessories. Almost immediately, he started working, and he was busy till it was closing time. As both Michael and Dev were residing in the same area in Vacoas, Dev gave him a lift in his car. Vacoas was proclaimed a town rather late in the day. It was town with the look of a well-developed village and the inhabitants were well mannered and quiet.

The following day, Michael came down to Port Louis with Dev, who had to come early to open the shop as the electrician wanted to start with his job as early in the day as possible.

"My cousin the mason will come to The Shop this morning. I convinced him to take a day's leave on the grounds that he is not feeling well," said Michael. Mauritian employees are well conversant with the idea of taking a day or two off on the pretext that they are not feeling well. They do it on any day, but more especially on Mondays, or on the eve of public holidays or on the day after the public holidays. In the latter case, they say that they are "doing the bridge", the meaning is clear. In most cases, the employee is not sick, he just wants to enjoy the day off or to work away from his employer. The employee keeps count of the number of sick leaves that he has taken at any given moment so that at the end of the year, he does not exceed his sick leave entitlement for which he is legally entitled. This applies both to the public sector as well as the private sector employees. Believe me, this art has been perfected over the years!

On the following day, the cousin of Michael did come and he agreed to complete the job on the same day provided he received the materials on the very day and he can get some help. The messenger-odd-job man of the premises was the handyman and driver and he went in the car of Dev to buy all the materials needed and around noon, with the help of the odd-job man, the mason started building the structure to house the generator. By six o'clock, it was ready but the mason said that it cannot be used immediately, it must be given time to dry out and this will take about three days.

Over the next two days, the electrician completed the rewiring of the whole premises and all he had to do now was to install the generator. The following day, Dev accompanied Michael to three different stores where they sell generators and at the last store, Dev decided to buy and take delivery of the wherewithal to produce electricity in case of need. The next day, the installation of the generator also was completed. When Dev decides to do something, anything for that matter, he has to do it as soon as possible, otherwise, he loses interest and then the decision would never be implemented.

Friends who came to the shop were happy to see that Dev had done, or rather caused to be done, so much within a matter of days. He told them that he was thinking of some violent cyclonic weather and he does not want to be taken by surprise when everybody will suffer from one crisis upon another.

The weather was as hot, if not hotter, as it had been during the previous week. When Michael completed the electrical work that he had undertaken, Dev called him in the office and offered him a drink.

"Sit down, Michael. We haven't had a chat for a long time now. How are the members of your family faring?" he asked, pouring two tots of rum and soda. And Dev placed a fistful of roasted nuts on a saucer to accompany the drink.

"They are alright, Mr Dev. My wife does some sewing if she can get a few clients. My elder daughter, the one you know, is married. But my son in law wants to stay with us and I honestly cannot tell him that this is not done, so I have to look after my daughter as well as her husband," Michael responded.

"I was given to understand that he does not have a regular employment and he does not earn a salary as such. He works on and off and therefore he gets some money on and off."

"That is the problem. He does not want to look for a regular job in some company or some firm, or even at the Municipality. You were a municipal councilor and then the mayor, if my son in law would have been interested to work even as a scavenger, I would have contacted you to get your help. I have come to the conclusion that it is useless to try to help him. My other daughter is taking some tuition but I don't think that she will be doing anything worthwhile. I think that it would be better for her also to get married and look after household duties and her husband." so opined Michael.

"That is the reason for you to work so hard, even when you are supposed to take a rest and enjoy yourself?"

"Well, you can say so, though the pension that I get is not enough for me and my family to lead a comfortable life. It is enough for me and my wife, but surely not enough for my younger daughter and the elder daughter as well as for her good for nothing husband. You think that I would not have appreciated taking a real rest after having worked for over forty five years without taking a holiday? I have had a very difficult life, with my father passing away before I was eight years old, my mother slaving morning till evening just to get some food and a shelter for my three brothers and two sisters. I have had to work since I was less than ten years old, and I have done it till now. And I am forced to do it even now. I also would have liked to go on holidays in other countries like others do, but that kind of ambition costs money, which I don't have. That is life for us. We have no choice but to accept what Fate has reserved for us, we cannot choose what we would prefer." After having said so much, the eyes of Michael became moist and he stopped speaking.

Dev also was quiet for some time, then he said, "You know, Michael, according to me, you should do your duty in life and do not bother about the results of what you do. If you can help any person who deserves your help, do oblige if you can and at the end of the day you will feel happy. Money comes and money goes, but do not think that those who have lots of money are more happy than you or me. I have a little bit of money in reserve, but you don't. That does not make me happier in life or that you don't have any money and that fact also does not make you more miserable in life. It is good to have some money in reserve; it ensures a certain degree of security in case you cannot work, or if you have to help a relative or a friend."

"I have never seen a lot of money nor will I ever see it. It's no use to think about it or to talk about it."

"One thing I will tell you, and it is this, do not ever be greedy about anything. Eat only the quantity that you can digest, if you over-eat, you are sure to get an indigestion. Remember what I am telling you today," said Dev.

"You are right Mister Dev, at times my eyes seem to be bigger than my belly."

"It's time to go, but I would like to tell you something before we proceed home. I would like you to drop by at my place say every two or three days, during the coming fortnight. You can have a look at the electric appliances at my place. You can come for only ten or fifteen minutes. Maybe I will need you for some other work, but I do not know yet whether it will materialize or not. Let's go now."

4. WILL THE CYCLONE COME TO US?

Two days after Dev had completed installing the generator in his shop, the weather was as hot as ever. He was thinking of going to India for a couple of weeks. He talked the matter over with his wife who was enthusiastic over the project, thinking that she had not been overseas on holidays for over three years. She loves going to India from time to time especially to go to the Temples to pray. She is a very religious person and she likes to drag Dev to all the places of pilgrimage that she visits. Dev voluntarily accompanies her, though he is not very sure where he stands in matters of religion. He does not believe so much in the rituals as in the philosophical aspect of Hinduism and he puts in practice what he believes in. He does not prevent Laxmi to indulge as much as she likes in the rituals, in fact he helps her in all the preparations, but in his heart of hearts, he believes only in the Vedanta aspect of Hinduism.

Dev was used to having his dinner in front of the television so that he could watch the news. When it came to news about the weather, the newscaster informed the viewers that a cyclone is in formation in the northeast of the country at a distance of twelve hundred kilometers but that at that moment it was not of interest to Mauritius. Dev talked to Laxmi. He said "I would very much like to go to India, and to tell you frankly the reason for such a decision is that I want to run away from the heat, at least for a couple of weeks. But if we shall be caught in a cyclone, I think that our plan should be postponed. We can't take the risk of leaving everything behind, especially The Shop, in a cyclone. And then we have the plantations."

Laxmi also was of the same opinion and said, "Let us put everything on hold for two weeks, then we shall decide. By that time we shall know how the cyclone is evolving."

The following day, Dev was in The Shop and he had a small transistor radio on his desk. He wanted to follow the evolvement of the cyclone and he learnt by the afternoon that a name has already been given to the newly formed cyclone. It was called Mady, a name chosen by the Malagasy Republic, for it was the turn of that country to name the cyclones of the Indian Ocean during that cyclonic period. Dev had nothing worthwhile to do, he was just thinking of the weather. He found it strange that cyclones are given exclusively feminine names, at least in our region. Why is it so? Cyclones cause havoc at times, bringing death and all sorts of miseries and destruction in their wake. Could this be the reason? He said to himself that he must find out the reason and especially about the person who has been responsible for such a blunder.

Though the weather was hot and humid as in the previous days, yet Dev was feeling still more restless in his shop and we went out of The Shop for a walk in the streets. A bit further from The Shop, there were several hawkers proposing their goods to the customers in loud voices. Some of them knew Dev and they greeted him and he also talked in a familiar manner to them.

Then he met somebody who knew him rather well and he wanted to sell something that Dev did not want. The hawker said, "Mr Dev, you do not recognize me? I am Kader, Long Kader you used to call me."

Dev knew so many people from Port Louis because he was born in the capital city, grew up there, he did his schooling there and used to be an active member of several clubs during his teens and he used to help his fellow citizens more than others.

Dev asked the hawker "Kader, where were you for so long? I haven't seen you for about two or three years. You have changed a lot and I would not have recognized you if you had not reminded me your name".

"What can I tell you, Mister Dev. Sooner or later, you will come to know. It is better for me to tell you rather than some other person would do so. You will then say that Long Kader has not played fair with Mister Dev. I do not want such a situation to develop between us. I was a guest of the Prime Minister and the government. I was very well treated, meals three times a day, plenty of rest and I was in the good books of the officers. They did not bother me and I did not bother them. It was the good life for me. How can I forget that I used to get a balanced diet, with a fruit with the meals and whenever I was feeling not very well, I was seen by a doctor. What more do you want? I ask you, can you tell me? They forced me to leave my nice cell and now I have to earn my living in this very hard way. What should I do to be the government's guest once more?"

"What offence did you commit last time?"

"You know the shop that is found near the Commercial Bank, the one that sells watches and perfumes? I broke into it at midnight about three years ago as I very badly wanted to have one of those watches. But I took ten of the watches; you agree with me that I may have been somewhat greedy. I sold nine of them, three to foreign tourists and five to locals and I gave one as a present to one of my cousins. I kept one for myself. A Police Officer saw the watch on my wrist and asked me where did I get it from?"

"Did you tell him that you had stolen it?"

"I will never do that. How can I put a noose around my own neck voluntarily? I asked the officer whether I couldn't buy such a watch? Would you believe me, he said loudly, no I cannot. He wanted to know where I had bought it from and how much did I pay for it. Then I was caught. This is the long and the short of my story."

"You know that now I have a shop opposite the Bank of Mauritius. I might need you one of these days. Where can I contact you?"

"I know where your shop is. Anytime you need me, I will be at your disposal."

Long Kader wrote down his phone number and handed it to Dev saying, "You know that I don't have a phone of the type the big people have. But I do have an ordinary mobile phone. Contact me on this number at any time except between one and two in the afternoon on Fridays. You know the reason, I can go against the law, but I cannot be against what I believe in."

When Dev returned to the shop, he found out that the cyclone was moving in a west-south-west direction at a speed of eight kilometres per hour. The direction of a cyclone is not fixed beforehand, at times it moves in a straight line, at other times in a loop or it goes in a southerly direction and then moves west or even east. People can expect the cyclone to pass far away from the country, but it can come very near to the country or pass directly over it. Some people say that when a cyclone reaches a certain distance from the country, the mountains have the power to attract it to the country, but people cannot vouch for this idea as they do not think that this is backed by any scientific study.

The speed at which the cyclone is travelling it would take about four to five days to reach us, that is if it passed near the country. Dev still had plenty of time to start thinking about his plan that could only be put in operation during the cyclone and that also only when the cyclone was big and deadly.

5. THE SLOWING DOWN OF TIME

That evening Dev listened with a greater attention to the weather bulletin broadcast on the television. He was not sure if the cyclone would pass over the country or not, it was as yet too far to make a more or less precise prediction. Even if the members of the scientific community would say that the cyclone would not approach the country, yet the cyclone could very well go against their calculations and pass over the country just to give a lie to their prediction, as if the cyclone did it on purpose.

Dev slept fitfully that night, he had been dreaming of a very strong cyclone hitting the country, all the wooden buildings were blown down and even his shop was damaged and people started looting his shop. He woke up in perspiration and had to get up, had a drink of water, but he could not get back to sleep. He went in his television room and watched a movie until it was morning.

At eight o'clock he went to his shop. On arriving there, he rang up Long Kader and asked him to come and meet him around five o'clock on the following day, if that was possible of course. Then he rang up Michael asked him to drop at his place at about seven o'clock on the same day. These arrangements completed, he met some friends in the office for some, what is popular known as, small talk. It was well known that Dev was a past master in indulging in small talk and for this reason, he was a well-appreciated person by those friends. What is small talk? Matters of gossip that will pin down the attention of those who are fond of such talk for some moment and some persons can spend hours in small talk. If we were to go further into the matter, it would be perceived that small talk is a form of relaxation for those who like it, so it was with Dev. Yet he was not feeling as relaxed as he would have liked, that is the reason for which he met some of his friends and the small talk relaxed him.

At around seven in the evening, Michael called on Dev. Dev asked him to walk with him to the place where they sell cigarettes and he so informed his wife Laxmi and both gentlemen went out. Dev was thinking how he could start talking on the subject that he considered rather delicate, but then decided that he had to do it somehow, so why wait?

"Don't you think that you have worked enough in your lifetime?"

"Of course I have worked for more than a lifetime; I have worked for my next life as well. But I have no choice. I have to live and so has my family. I do not want them to suffer from malnutrition as did my mother. I still remember what kind of life my mother was leading when my father passed away. You understand the reason for my still working so hard". So said Michael.

Dev bought his cigarettes and they came back. He did not feel that he had enough courage to start talking to Michael about the subject for which he had called him. Dev said, "I want to discuss with you about a subject on which I wanted to talk to you, but I do not think that the time is ripe yet. Maybe I will do it the next time we shall meet. By the way, when will you be coming to Port Louis?"

"I have to buy materials that is needed for the house of a client of mine. I am supposed to go to Port Louis for that purpose, and I can do it tomorrow itself. Is the subject that you want to discuss important?"

"I would say so. I will see you in The Shop tomorrow at about five o'clock, after you would have bought the materials. In this way you will get a lift to come back home".

"This will be the ideal situation for me."

"You can also have a look at the generator. It is emitting too much smoke. I do not like it."

"I can do that tomorrow, for that I would have to be there somewhat earlier, around four thirty." With that they parted company.

When Dev came back, Laxmi asked him about Michael. Dev told her, "The generator at the shop is emitting too much smoke and I do not like it. I called him to find out what should be done. So he is coming to The Shop tomorrow. The cyclone is coming in our direction and we should buy the necessary provision. You must make a list of the provisions that we need and we can buy them tomorrow."

The following morning Dev followed in the newspaper the direction that the cyclone was taking but it was not possible to predict the route that it will eventually follow. The weather was still hot and humid and there was no sign that the country will be experiencing a heavy downpour soon. There was no breeze to give some sort of a relief from the heat. What was in store for the people within the next seven days? That was what thinking persons were wondering about.

Dev arrived at The Shop and instructed his employees to see to it that there was nothing that needed to be repaired and if there was, it had to be repaired immediately, before the cyclone hit them. "We do not want to be taken by surprise. This shop is the prime source of our livelihood, for all of us and we do not want that the source gets damaged or dries up," so he said. Soon the employee who could afford it, inspected the building, especially the structural part and the openings and he found that one or two openings needed tightening and he tightened them by himself, the concrete roof was in good condition and there was no fear of springing a leak.

That was the first cyclone since Dev had purchased the shop and he did not have the experience of managing a business concern. He had done rather well when the weather was fine, but now he had to see how he would manage when there was a cyclone. However, he had enough common sense and he had the intelligence to make a success of whatever plan he formulated.

In front of everyone, Dev was the jolly fellow that he had always been. Cracking a joke here, giving a piece of advice there, talking about some serious subject at a third place and also talking of the impending effects of the cyclone. But Dev was facing a problem and he could not talk about this problem to anybody, not even to his wife Laxmi who was the repository of nearly all his secrets. There was one Dev that was meant for everybody, but there was another Dev who was known but to himself.

Dev knew that he was intelligent, maybe more intelligent than his friends, at least most of them, though he did not have the certificates to prove what he was worth. He knew that he had wasted his time when he had to study, he had all the facilities to make a good show at every institution he joined, but somewhere and somehow he went astray. These happenings in his life irked him, more than he realized. He would have liked to be as the other persons who were his friends and who had succeeded in life in spite of being far less intelligent than himself. Even most of his relatives have been successful in their careers and Dev has to put up with the side remarks made by them. It is easy to say that you do not care for the opinion of others to whoever you like, but when you are alone, it is difficult to digest what you know and hear, especially as you know that you yourself are the cause of all your problems.

Sitting at his table, Dev was thinking of one particular incident in his life. When he had come back from his supposed studies in Europe, he got a scholarship, courtesy of the then Chief Minister of the country, who was later to become the Prime Minister. His family was well known to the Chief Minister, as were so many other politicians. It happened that Dev came across the Chief Minister by chance and the Chief Minister said, "What are you doing these days?"

"Nothing much, sir, but I think that I will be taking a job soon," replied Dev.

"Why don't you become a journalist? I know you can do well in this profession with a little bit of luck and some hard work. See me sometime next week."

"I will do that. Thank you very much."

Dev went to see the Chief Minister as requested. Now the Chief Minister was the leader of the main political party in the country. About ten years previously, he had founded a newspaper to air the views of his party, and he was keeping a close watch of its progress. Without much ado, he told Dev, "If you are interested to make a career in journalism, you can get a scholarship to study the profession for one year. I will talk to my contacts at the well-known French newspaper *Le Monde* where you will understudy one of my friends. Would you be agreeable to this suggestion?"

"Can I think over the matter and talk it over to my wife and let you know by tomorrow?"

"Of course do that. How is your wife? I have not seen her brother for more than a year. You know he is a good friend of mine. By the way, how is your father? I take it that he is still busy with his profession. We don't meet these days because I have a very tight schedule of work. Give my regards to all these persons and one day as soon as I am free, I will make it a point to see them. The attachment that I have with them cannot be described. I will see you tomorrow."

Dev talked the matter over with his wife, Laxmi, and managed to convince her that he had the chance of a lifetime to be attached to *Le Monde* and this cannot be brushed aside. She was just expecting that Dev will take the attachment at *Le Monde* really seriously and he will settle down and lead a normal life with a steady job. Dev knew that this was what she was thinking but she did not tell him anything, so much the better for him.

In France, Dev studied journalism during twenty five percent of the time when he was supposed to devote a hundred percent, the rest of the time was spent on other useless activities like going to the races. He used to bet regularly on the horses that lost the races but he was not concerned with these petty matters. At the end of the year, he returned to the country and he was employed in the newspaper of the Chief Minister. He used all his contacts to promote the paper and he was doing much more than journalism. He was doing so many things that he used to lose track of many of his activities. All of a sudden, he became fed up of his work as a journalist and so he left his job.

His work as a journalist had brought him close to one of the trade unionists in the sugar industry. He became his assistant but in fact he was guiding the unionist. They called for a strike. Dev was very busy going from this estate to that, giving all types of instructions to the workers. At the end of the day, the management of the estates concerned called the trade unionist for negotiation. And of course the trade unionist was accompanied with Dev. The managers were surprised that a person like Dev was negotiating on behalf of the workers. In fact, Dev could talk with the managers on an equal footing, be it in language terms, on the economic front or on the rights of the workers. He was the only trade unionist who was better in the spheres where the managers considered themselves better. Dev showed them that negotiation is on issues and not on persons. And the managers were forced to concede to most of the demands of the workers.

And as always Dev gave up trade unionism and turned to politics. But that is a different story. He was impatiently waiting for time to pass. He was feeling hot and the humidity in the atmosphere was increasing his discomfort. He preferred to take a walk, had some fast food by the road side, he took two pairs of Dal Puris and then came back to The Shop. Outside it was still warmer than inside. But time for him had slowed down as if to make him suffer for longer than ever.

PART II –EXECUTION

6. THE CYCLONE IS NEARLY UPON US

At long last it was 4.30 pm. And Michael came. Dev took him to the office and closed the door. They sat down. Dev started by saying, "Another person is supposed to see me at around five o'clock. We do not have much time."

"What do you have to tell me Mr Dev?"

"I have a proposal, a project in which I would like to include you. It is risky and it is dangerous. It is against the law. But in the end it will be worth the risk and the danger. If you accept you must keep your mouth shut, you must not talk of the project to your wife, to your children or to your other relatives and friends. You must trust me. If you agree, you must tell me. If not let us just forget that we ever talked about this."

That was the introduction of Dev. Michael was dumbfounded for two minutes. Eventually, he said, "I thank you for having included me in your project. I trust you completely and have faith in your project whatever it can be."

"I will tell you in greater detail in half an hour's time. The other person will come and I will ask him whether he will join us and if he accepts, we shall plan our strategies together. In the meantime, you can have a look at the generator which is emitting too much smoke."

They went outside where the generator was housed and Michael was busy with the apparatus and Dev went inside the shop. Soon, Long Kader came, somewhat earlier than it was convened. Anyway, Dev took him in the office and closed the door.

"Sit down, Kader. Listen to what I have to tell you. If you will agree to what I will tell you, we can move ahead. Otherwise, just tell me that you do not agree with what I intend to propose and we shall just forget what I am telling you. I have a project that is dangerous and risky. It is also illegal. But you will not be the loser. You know me well enough and that since you were a child. I have known your father who was working on a regular basis for my father."

"Mr Dev, I know you very well. I have full trust in you and in your capacities and you have never let down any person who has done something for you. Without asking you what your project involves, I am saying right now, that I will be with you. If you can trust me, count me in, you just have to order me what to do," Kader said.

Dev continued, "I thank you, Kader. But you must not talk about the project to even those who are close to you. Not even to your mother, because I know that you have no brothers or sisters and your father died some years back. I have thought of all these matters before I included you in the plan."

After some time, Michael came in the office and he said Hello to Kader and to Dev he said "Mr Dev, there is nothing wrong with the generator. I have made some adjustments and it will not emit so much smoke now."

Dev invited him to have a seat and he said, "Michael, may I introduce to you Kader? He performs different jobs depending on the circumstances. He is a person to get you out of some difficult situation. Kader, I introduce you to Michael. By profession he is an electrician and a good one at that." They said hello to each other and that was that. They did not have any further conversation. Dev left them alone in the office and went in the shop. He told the employees that they may close The Shop and that he will go home some time later. And they took a quarter of an hour to close the shop. Dev asked them about the weather and he was told that the cyclone is approaching the country but slowly, at about ten kilometres per hour. When they left, Dev locked the door from inside and went in the office to join his two acquaintances.

Dev noticed that Michael and Kader were talking of the cyclone and the possibility and probability of it approaching the country in such a way that it will become a danger to the country and its inhabitants. Dev brought three glasses and a jug of water. And he removed a bottle of whisky from a cabinet. He poured whisky for all three and each of them mixed the whisky with water and said, "Cheers" and each took a sip. Dev had not asked Kader whether he drank alcoholic beverages or not, he just assumed that he did. Then Dev started to tell them the reason for their being in the shop.

He said, "Both of you are here at my request. Both of you know me, I also know you but you do not know each other. I have a project which I would like executed. As I told you the plan is not without risk and it is dangerous. But it is simple to execute if we follow the rules.

"We have to enter into a bank, remove a fixed sum of money in the form of bank notes, not new but second hand. We break into the bank, remove the notes and retire quietly. I know that it sounds impossible to do what I am proposing."

The other two were thinking that Dev is losing his head for proposing such a dangerous crime.

Kader said "Mr Dev, what you are proposing can never be done successfully. We shall all end up our days in prison. I have been inside, and in spite of what I told you the other day, I think of my mother, she has made me take an oath that I will not do anything that will land me in prison once more. I really think that you have not thought well about your plan."

Michael had listened quietly to Kader. He said "Let us listen a bit more to what Mr Dev has to say. Then we can make up our minds. How are you going to execute your plan? Give us some more details."

Dev told them, "I know that it is more or less impossible to break into a bank. Can you imagine that I will expose myself together with you to the risk of being caught breaking into a bank? Do you think that I am ready to take the risk of being caught by the Police, judged by the Court and sentenced to a term of imprisonment? No relative of mine has had to undergo such a humiliating treatment, why would I be the first? Just listen to me. We must make a fool proof plan and we must work hard for it. If we plan well, we are bound to succeed. Our main ally would be nothing but Nature, I mean the forthcoming cyclone, provided it comes to visit our island. The stronger it will be the better for us."

"How can the cyclone help us? I know that there is no activity during the cyclonic period, nobody is out of his house because there is the risk of losing life for no reason." so responded Kader.

"Why do you think I bought this shop two years ago, I refurbished it and re-arranged everything and now it is going on better than I would have ever thought? Do you think I was interested in The Shop or to become a shopkeeper, be tied day in day out to look after a shop? I have been thinking for over two years about my plan.

"I have been waiting for such an occasion for long enough and now I think that opportunity is ready to smile at me. We can have a cyclone that will be very strong and the eye will pass right over the country. If these conditions would not be met, I am sorry to say that we would not be able to proceed.

"If the cyclone were to hit us directly and if it is strong enough, in that case only we can do our work." Dev said.

Then he put the radio on to listen to news about the cyclone. He continued, "Are you interested to be with me or do you want to stay away from what I am proposing? At the end of the day, you will receive ten million rupees each, not a cent more. But the difficult thing would be to manage those ten million. Believe me; it is not easy to manage such a sum by people living like you. If you will not talk about the matter to anybody, I really mean to anybody, and if there is not a dramatic change in your lifestyle, I can guarantee that you will not be caught.

"The problem with criminals is that they boast of their activities with their friends and relatives. They change their life style and neighbours and friends and relatives start putting to themselves questions. Criminals can't shut their mouths and sooner than later, they are caught. Police officers have their informers everywhere."

Kader interrupted him. "I agree with you that I have been caught by the Police only when I have talked to my friends or I have started living differently. Now I understand that I should have stayed quiet. Nobody would have been any wiser."

Michael was already thinking what he would do with the million rupees that he had the chance of receiving. Plans were being made in his head and he was elated. He woke from his reverie and he heard Dev saying that there is not much time for the cyclone to hit the country. "We must be ready by the day after tomorrow at latest, so we must start now. Time is very short but we must make do with what time we have."

Michael asked "What are we supposed to do?"

Dev replied, "Both of you should go to the Mauritius Planters Bank tomorrow, to have a look inside, get the feel and have a *reconnaissance des lieux* sort of. You must not make it obvious of course. You do not know each other and each of you will be there for a different purpose. Michael you can go there in order to try to get a loan. You can tell the officer that you want to set up a company to service the electricity sector. You can tell him what your qualifications are and the work experience that you have. Can you do it?"

"Of course I can. I have some experience in such matters. I was at the Bank in Quatre Bornes where I do my transactions. I was there for a loan, but there is no need to tell you that I did not get the loan for certain reasons. I had wanted to borrow not a big sum, only one hundred thousand rupees but even then they refused, maybe they did not like my face."

"What about you, Kader? What would be your pretext to go to that bank?"

"I do not need any pretext. I have a small account at that bank. I can go there to verify my account and to deposit another sum. I go there nearly every fortnight for my transaction, though my transaction never exceeds one thousand rupees. I know so many persons there and they know me as well." That was the answer of Kader.

"Keep an eye on the cyclone's movement, listen to the news bulletin and you Kader, must get us three pair of gloves, thin ones, like the doctors use. You, Michael, you must get ready with your electrical tools and both of you should think of what we would need to get inside the bank and in the strong room and in the vault. Do not give any hint to anybody about what we intend to do. You must move about normally as you have been doing every day. At the end of the day, you will be happy.

"I think that is all for today. I shall see you tomorrow. Remember the cyclone is approaching our country, it can gather speed or it can slow down and it can come in a straight line or it can move in a zigzag manner or it can make a loop. We cannot be sure of its movement; we depend entirely on its movement and what it is reserving for us nobody can say."

Kader left and Dev told Michael that he would drop him in Vacoas and they could talk a little bit more in the car. As soon as Dev was getting into his car, somebody called him, "Mr Dev, you are going home? If so, can you give me a lift if you don't mind."

That person was a neighbor of his and Dev could not refuse giving him a lift. Dev asked him how is the weather and he said, "The cyclone is fast approaching and despite the fact that it will soon be night, it is still so hot. We were waiting for some rain but not a cyclone. If the cyclone approaches us, it will destroy all the standing crops, we shall be deprived of vegetables and our markets would not be functioning, we shall be bound to import even tomatoes and cabbages and chillies and what not. But people would have no money to buy them and that will be the problem. Then so many houses would be blown down, people would be housed in the cyclone shelters and all our schools would be used for that purpose. Do not talk of the number of deaths, thinking of the cyclone makes me shudder. So why talk of the impending danger? Let us hope that the cyclone does not come near us, but of course we must pray for some rain."

Dev could not talk to Michael in the car and when he reached home, he remembered that he had promised his wife

Laxmi that he would take her shopping for the items needed during a cyclone. So they went to a shopping mall and Dev just accompanied Laxmi who did the shopping. Dev appeared preoccupied, his wife noticed it but she thought that the time was not appropriate to ask him about it while they were shopping. When they were having dinner Laxmi said, "Is something bothering you? You appear preoccupied and you are not talking as you used to do."

He said, "What is bothering me is this cyclone. We shall all suffer, and I don't like suffering nor do I like to see other people suffering. Besides, this is the first time that we have The Shop in a cyclone, we do not know if it will resist the cyclonic gusts which might reach up to three hundred kilometres per hour. I am afraid thieves would be prowling around and we can never know their intention. In case of an interruption of electricity, the generator that Michael has installed can help us. All these matters are bothering me. Thank God, our house is strong enough to withstand gusts of winds of over three hundred kilometres per hour so at least I do not have to worry about the house getting damaged. We have candles, the torch, enough food to last us about a month, two cylinders of gas that will last two months and some bottled water. So we have the essentials, and that there is no need to go out of the house during and immediately after the cyclone. You must keep your telephone fully charged until there is electricity in the house. These are some of the elementary precautions that you should take during the cyclonic period. I know that you are well aware of what I am telling you, but I am doing it just to remind you."

Laxmi listened to Dev but did not make any remark. The television was on and now it was time for the weather bulletin and both Dev and Laxmi listened with particular attention. "The cyclone has now slowed down to six kilometres per hour. Normally, when a cyclone slows down, it gathers momentum and strength and becomes a bigger and more violent cyclone." Dev knows this from experience and he doesn't talk about it from having read in some book. And Laxmi also.

Dev said, "If we will have to face a really violent cyclone, I think I will stay in the shop."

Laxmi did not wait for him to say anything further. She said, "You cannot do that. You cannot leave your house, what will happen to me, to us, alone in the cyclone? You cannot just think of your shop. When the second cyclone warning is issued, you must close the shop and come back home. What will people say? And then you will be alone in the shop. You know how I would feel thinking of you? You will not have any food for I do not know how many hours, do you think that I will be able to eat, thinking that you are hungry?"

Dev was quietly listening to Laxmi. He knew that she was right but how to convince her that he had to be in the shop? That was a problem that he would have to face very soon.

He tried to talk nicely to her. "Alright, if you so feel, but at the same time I cannot leave the shop without a watchman especially during the cyclone."

"Why don't you look for a watchman tomorrow?"

"You think that it is that easy? And then the watchman himself might turn out to be the biggest thief. We do not have that much time for that type of exercise. I am thinking… I might ask Michael to help me in that. Provided he can do it and provided there is no objection from his family. You know, he is a good husband and a good father."

"I know that and you must follow his example. By the way, how is your generator functioning? I think we must have one here also." Such was Laxmi's response. Dev then said "at the first opportunity, we shall cause a generator to be installed to service the house. It can be done in a day or two. The first day, we shall need the services of a mason and when the work of the mason has dried, Michael can install the generator."

Dev watched the television channel of La Reunion and then the international channel the CNN, to get further news of the cyclone. The cyclone was still moving slowly and there was a fear of it is still strengthening. And going awry.

Dev, that night again, did not get a peaceful sleep, he kept dreaming of the cyclone and robbers and of his shop. He woke up early, before Laxmi, which was contrary to his habit.

7. THE PLAN IS BEING FINALISED

Dev asked one of his employees how was the cyclone moving? The employee replied, "it has taken a west-north-west direction. It appears that it has changed course and now I have the impression that it will start going away from us."

But then during the day, it slowed down yet further, and the meteorology people were saying that the cyclone is more or less stationary. They said that they will issue a further bulletin by three o'clock in the afternoon. Dev gave instructions to his employees what should be done if the cyclone decided to hit them. "When the authorities will issue a Class III warning the shop must be closed. The windows must be well secured, and the main door as well. I do not have a watchman for the shop, but I have decided to request Michael, the electrician to be in the shop during the time that the cyclone would be with us. I hope that he will accept to cooperate with us."

Dev went to one of the Chinese shops that he knew well where he could get a good torchlight. He talked to the owner about the cyclone, and decided to buy two torches. He returned to the shop because outside it was really hot. He was listening to the radio when the newscaster informed the listeners that the cyclone had started moving in the west-south-west direction after having made a loop and now it appeared that the danger for the country was becoming real and precise. If it maintained that trajectory, there was a real possibility that it would pass slightly to the western part of the country, at about fifty kilometers from the west coast.

The newscaster said, "We have been informed that the cyclone is an intense one with a huge diameter. If it will hit the country directly, we can expect lots of damages and if people are not careful there might be loss of life as well. Those who live in houses that are not well conditioned and well secured, are advised to think of moving into cyclone refugee shelters. We shall now give you a list of such shelters. We advise those who think of moving in the cyclone refugee shelters should secure their belongings and lock the doors of their houses."

And a list of schools that had been declared as cyclone refugee shelters were read out. Many persons from the *cites* were getting ready to move in the refugee shelters. It is interesting to find out who are the persons who take refuge in the shelters. Some of them do live in squatter settlements, and once they move in these shelters, they do not want to move out unless they are given a house. This is pure blackmail. The others also do not want to go back to their houses because so long as they stay in the shelters, they are given some food and some allowance. Getting those in the shelters out of the schools becomes a headache to the authorities. The schools that are under the occupation of people who have no right to be there cannot be used for the purpose for which they were built, that is schools. Dev was musing on those types of people, but by then, Michael arrived.

"Come in, Michael. I have to talk to you about the cyclonic weather." They went in the office. Dev continued. "You know that the likelihood of the cyclone coming directly on us is getting more and more precise. When all the persons I meet are looking worried, I am glad at heart, but I must act and behave like the other persons. It is not difficult to do that, you know.

"We must be here in the midst of the cyclone. So I am saying to the persons who matter that you will stay here during the cyclone, as a sort of watchman. You must convince your wife that you have to do it. I tried to tell my wife that I will stay in The Shop during the cyclone, but she is dead against. But I will manage to convince her."

Kader arrived. He said, "I have done my duty. Here are the gloves. I have brought six pairs in case we would need them. I also went to the bank; I talked to several persons as I always do. I have been able to find out where the strong room is located. To open the strong room would be very difficult and I do not know if we can get access to the vault."

Michael said, "I also have been to the bank with the idea of having a loan. The officer asked me many questions, as if I will get the loan. He has given me some forms to fill in. I think that I will do that and wait for the outcome. I had a look around, I tried to locate the CCTV cameras, the alarm and its connections and the entrance. Of course at the bank they have a big generator and as soon as the central electricity goes off, the generator starts within seconds."

"Do they have watchmen inside the bank when a cyclone is blowing in full force? If they have, the watchmen will be our main obstacle to carry out our plan."

"I think they have two watchmen, both inside because we can't expect them to be walking outside," said Kader.

Then Dev asked him he must get three stockings, women's I mean. You can get them tomorrow, I suppose?"

"There is no problem. My friend sells them; he is a street hawker, same as me."

"Each one of us must have a clean handkerchief with us. Now Kader, you have to look after the necessary tools to enter in the strong room as well as in the safe.

"However, the most important part would come after we have succeeded in our enterprise. Each of you will receive only ten million rupees, not a cent more, not a cent less. I am saying this because I know that when you will see all the money in the vault, you will get the urge to remove as much as you can carry. I would want you to be reasonable. I do not want you to get caught by the Police.

"How are you going to spend that money? That will be a problem for you to manage. You cannot start spending as soon as you get the money. If you would accept my advice, I will say that your life must not change before six months. Later on, you will understand the reason for my saying so. I am thinking of the work you now do, whether you pay tax on your revenue and other matters.

"I will remove thirty million rupees for myself. You must be wondering why I'll be keeping thirty million when I have said that each of you will be receiving ten million. The reason is very simple. I will not spend a cent of that money. I am removing that money for a specific reason; I will keep it in a safe and secure place. You must trust me on my honour. Later on, I will tell you why I am doing this. I am telling you that I am not doing this for my benefit. Maybe I will tell you later the reason. Be patient, for patience is a virtue which few persons have.

"I have not hidden anything from you. Why have I included Michael in the project? The reason is that I have studied his way of living. At heart, he is a good man. He has always worked hard and he has never spent more than he has earned. He has a few tots of rum nearly every day, but he is not a drunkard. I do think that he deserves better than what life has provided for him. So I thought that if I could help him to have a second chance in life, why not give him that chance? I have tried to help him otherwise, he knows it very well.

"Now about you, Kader, I know you since you were a small boy, you used to come with your father and your mother when they used to work for my parents. I and my brother used to talk to you, we were telling you all sorts of funny stories, we were teaching you how to swear, how to use the biggest swear words. We used you instruct you not to tell your father what we were teaching you. But we knew that you were repeating to him all the swear words that we were teaching you. We thought that we were doing you a favor. I know that you were not interested in your studies and early in life your father put you as an apprentice in the mechanical sector with a motor mechanic. I always tried to help you when you were growing up. Then your father passed away, leaving you and your mother alone. You were not interested in a mechanic's work. You left the garage, you did some odd jobs but you became acquainted with some people living on the fringe of society. You became a sort of specialist in small-time larceny and breaking and entering. You have been to prison several times; you are what is technically called a habitual criminal. As from now on, I would like you to follow the path of reform and to think of your mother. Don't you think that she has suffered enough in life because of you?

"Can I ask both of you one question that will affect your future life?"

That was what Dev told them. Both of them readily agreed to whatever Dev said. Dev then continued, "Where would you keep your share of the proceeds? You do not have houses big enough where you can keep the money in secret. You might get the temptation to start spending as soon as you will receive it. You, Kader, can your house resist a cyclone? You Michael, what about your family when they will know that you have that much money? They will talk and sooner or later, news of your money will reach the ears of the Police. And that will be the end of all three of us. I have a plan for each of you, and if you agree to follow my advice and directives, I will disclose it to you. But that will come later."

Kader said, "To tell you frankly, I am tired of leading the life that I have been leading since my father passed away. Do you think that I would not have liked to get a regular job, have a good house and look well after my mother? Up to now I have not been able to do so only because of myself. Maybe I was not provided with the proper guidance when it was most needed. I am not blaming anybody for that, mind you. The blame lies solely on me."

Kader added, "I agree that I cannot keep the money at my place. A solution must be found and quickly."

"All three of us must meet here again tomorrow and depending on the movement of the cyclone, it is possible that we shall have to spend the night in The Shop. But we do not know yet." With that Dev concluded the so-called meeting.

The weather was still hot and humid and many people were expecting the cyclone to reach the country soon, then the temperature of the weather will go down. The three persons parted company, but two minutes later, Michael came back and asked Dev whether he will go to Vacoas and if yes could he have a lift? Dev answered positively to both questions.

Michael said "I was thinking of visiting my cousin, but I have changed my mind. It would be better for me to go straight home, I might have to prepare for the project."

8....PREPARING TO MEET THE CYCLONE HEAD ON

The news bulletin of the weather was assuring for Dev, though not so to the majority of the Mauritians. People were advised to start consolidating their houses. They were told to stock the necessary provisions, candles, matches and other essentials. The newscaster added, "The Meteorological Services have informed us that cyclone Mady has a wide diameter and the wind outside the eye is very strong indeed. We can say that it is one of the strongest cyclones to hit the country in living memory. That is the reason for which we are appealing to the population earnestly to be prepared both physically and mentally to face Mady and at the same time have a thought for the neighbours. There is a cyclone warning Class II in force." And the warning was repeated twice. Then the list of cyclone refugee shelters was read over once more. The cyclone was still at a distance of about six hundred kilometres and Dev still had some time to make further arrangements about his plan.

He talked to his wife about Michael staying in the shop during the cyclone. He said "I talked to Michael. He informed me that he will have to talk to the members of his family first, but in so far as he is concerned, he has no objection. By tomorrow morning he will let me know of the position."

"What would you do if he refuses?"

"I really do not know what I will do. Do you think that it will be a good idea to ask Neela to come and stay with you during the cyclone? After all she stays alone, she is of a certain age and she has worked for us for about fifteen years. You will be doing her a favour and in her turn, she can help you during the cyclone with the cooking and some household duties and she will not have to wait for the cyclone to be really gone before she thinks of moving out of her house."

"The idea is not bad. She stays alone in that house which in my opinion is not that strong. I will tell her tomorrow. But you must think what you will do for a watchman for the shop."

Laxmi went to bed but Dev stayed awake. He was silently praying that the mountains of the country were high enough to attract the cyclone right over the country. This will give him the opportunity to better put his plan in execution. If he will miss putting it in execution during this cyclone, it means that he will never do it.

He was also thinking of the two persons who will be with him. Are they trustworthy? Anyway, it is too late to backtrack. He will have to trust them as they have trusted him. So far as his searches go, he has not found anything that makes them to be untrustworthy people. Has he not counted his chickens before they were hatched? Well only time will tell: And time is at our door step.

He went in the garage where he used to keep odds and ends. He had a piece of string made of nylon, about six metres long. He put it in his bag. Then there was a bottle of some sort of a liquid and he put this also in the bag. There was another small bottle with a differently coloured liquid. This bottle was in a small box filled with cotton and Dev was handling the box as if with kid gloves. He secured it separately in the boot of the car. There were some sticks of dynamite in a small bag which was well secured. This he secured in the boot of his car as well. Lastly, he had a ladder made of nylon ropes and wooden bars. He tied it well and put it in his bag. The bag was already half full.

Dev always had his Swiss Army knife in the car. He put it in his bag as well. He had all that he needed and he hoped that the others had collected what they had to in order that the operation will be successful. Dev then went to bed but he could not sleep. Laxmi woke up and asked Dev why isn't he sleeping?

He said, "I don't feel like it. I am thinking of the cyclone and of The Shop. What would I do in case Michael were to refuse to stay in the shop during the cyclone? We have invested so much money and so much effort has gone into it to make it what it is today. A cyclone comes and the risk that we might lose everything that the shop represents is very real. Anyway, go back to sleep. I'll go and watch some television programme. I shall come back to bed later." He watched an old Indian film, of maybe the fifties. It was entitled CID. Laxmi came to sit with Dev and she also started watching the film. And they watched it till the end.

Dev woke up the following morning very early. He made a cup of tea and was listening to the radio. When the news came he was all ears. The first item was, as expected, about the cyclone. It was moving at a speed of nine kilometres per hour in a south-west-south direction and was then located at about three hundred kilometres from the northern tip of the country. Because of the intensity of the cyclone and of its size, the risk that Mauritius will suffer from a calamity is increasing by the hour. If the cyclone will pass right through the country, which means to say that the eye will pass over the country, the risk of danger will be far greater.

When Laxmi came in the kitchen, Dev told her about the cyclone, and obviously she was concerned. Then there was a phone call. It was Michael and he informed him, that his wife did not want him to be out of the house because she thought that he might go somewhere he should not or he might be going out with friends for a drinking party. He told Dev to talk to his wife and tell her where he would be.

He talked to the wife and she asked him if he will be at the shop as well. He was in a dilemma. He told Michael's wife that he will ring her up in ten minutes. He then talked to his wife and told her what the wife had said. "It will look bad if I would send her husband to watch over The Shop whilst I will be at home." But Laxmi had the solution. She said "Provided you are not alone during the cyclone, I will have no objection, but only on the express condition that Michael will be with you."

"What about you? I know that we have our son and his family as well as our daughter and her family who stay close to us. They have their own houses and their families to look after. You will be alone here, but no, Neela will keep you company. Do you think that it will be alright?"

"Do not bother about me. As you have the habit of saying that our house is strong, that it can withstand any cyclone, where is the problem? But you take care of yourself and stay inside the shop, do not get out in the cyclone. When everything is over, only then you can come out."

"Do not forget to keep your portable phone fully charged; I will ring you up every three or four hours to find out about the situation."

"I will prepare some food that you can take with you. You can take a few packets of biscuit, some juice and you must also not forget your medicines."

That was the conversation between Dev and Laxmi. Dev then rang up Michael and informed him that he will accompany him in the shop, his wife need not fear for him. Michael informed his wife and it was arranged that they will go to the shop at about nine o'clock.

In the meantime there was another cyclone bulletin. "We are informing our listeners that a class III warning is in force in the country. The latest observation indicates that cyclone Mady has gathered further momentum and it is becoming a very big cyclone. It is still moving at a speed of nine kilometres per hour, and it is still in a south-south-west direction. If it will not change course, it will pass directly over the country. In such a case, the eye of the cyclone will give a false sense of security that the cyclone has moved away after the first phase. People normally think that the cyclone has really moved away from the country, but they do not realize that it becomes more dangerous when the other part, the tail end so to say will pass over us. We have to emphasize that it is very dangerous to be out of your house or other shelter when the eye is passing over the country. You will experience an extreme calmness, giving you a feeling of false freedom, a false sense of security. You must take all the necessary precaution to avoid being injured or worse."

Other news about the eventual hitting of the country by the cyclone followed; then the list of the cyclone refugee centres followed, after which this piece of news was given. "We have just been informed that around noon, a fresh bulletin of cyclone Mady will be issued. In the meantime all precautions must be taken. The Ministry of Education has already informed parents that there will be no school today. Children should not be allowed to stay outdoors."

The atmosphere was heavy so to say, hot and humid, as if waiting for some misfortune to fall upon everybody. But everybody was not having the same feeling. Some were more concerned, but for different reasons. Some were thinking of their business, some about their plantation, some about their family, some about the coups that they were planning to execute, some about their loved ones that they will not be able to meet and some for some other reason.

Around nine o'clock, Michael came and Dev got ready to go. He put the food in the boot of the car. Laxmi told him to be careful and not to take any risk. She gave Dev a big flask of tea.

Dev was in the shop around a quarter to ten. He asked the employees about the cyclone and then he told them that they should take particular care of their family. He further enquired about the condition of the houses in which they were living. One was a tenant in a building that was not that strong, but he could not say what may happen. Another had his own house and he said, "My house is a concrete building and I have already offered to accommodate Raj and his family during the cyclone. He can send his wife as well as his two children to my place right now; he can come just before the cyclone. He does not seem to realize the danger that his family will be facing. I do not live far from him, he knows my house. Besides, my wife knows his wife; they are members of the same Temple. There will be no problem."

Dev told the tenant employee that if his house was really not strong enough to withstand the cyclone, he must move with his family to the place of his friend. "Now it is not the time to think of your personal dignity or what will people say. You have a duty towards your family and your first duty is to them."

The third employee was living in a joint family in a very big house and Dev was told, "My house is secure. When there is a cyclone, it is a sort of festival for all the kids. You know there are more than thirty children in our house. There are always some persons to look after them."

If a foreigner were to visit Mauritius, he would get the impression that Mauritians are obsessed with cyclones. This does happen when a cyclone is very near to them. They have lived through many cyclones, they know their effects and after effects and the misery that they cause. Everybody then lives for the cyclone of the day, talks about it especially how they can help each other. "You must live during the cyclone to get the real feeling, nobody can describe it second hand," as they say, and rightly so. Some tourists stay in the country just to live through a good cyclone, as if there is such a phenomenon as a good cyclone, and most of such tourists go back home satisfied that they have seen Nature in its other aspect.

9....WAITING FOR THE EVENT TO START

Around noon, Long Kader arrived and he was closely followed by Michael who had left his bag in the shop with Dev. Kader told Dev that his mother had sent some Dal Puris for him because she knows that he appreciates them. Dev and Michael were eating the Dal Puris when there was news about the cyclone on the radio. It started, "A class III warning is in force in Mauritius. At eleven thirty today, the meteorological services have taken the decision to issue a Class III warning. Cyclone Mady is approaching close to the country and if it will continue on the same trajectory that it has taken since last night, it will hit the country directly, which will make it much more dangerous than otherwise. We are thinking of upgrading the warning to a class IV warning around five o'clock this evening. People are advised to complete all preparations. We shall come up with an hourly bulletin, so far as it will be possible."

Dev left the office, went in the shop proper and called all the three employees. He told them "as there is a Class III warning in force, it is time to close The Shop. So lock up, see that all the windows and the main door are well closed and locked. Be very careful during the cyclone and I shall see you when the cyclone has left us."

One of the employees asked him when will he go home to which he replied, "I cannot leave the shop with only Michael as a watchman during the cyclone. I will have to stay here at least tonight."

All three employees replied that this cannot be. How can they stay at home while will be in this place in the very violent cyclone? They said that he should allow them to make the necessary arrangements for one of them to stay in The Shop.

Dev was touched by the solicitation of the employees. He told them that there was no need to, because Michael, the electrician had agreed to stay provided he is not alone, that is a condition imposed by his wife. My wife also did not want me to stay here all alone with the cyclone howling outside. But she agreed when I told her that the electrician will be with me. So complete what you have to do and you can go home."

In the streets people were rushing to go home or to do some late shopping. Dev asked Kader to go to the Central Market and purchase some bread, some cakes, some juice, butter, cheese whatever he will see of interest to eat during the cyclone. In half an hour, the employees had already left and soon Kader was back with the food. The front door was locked, lights were put off except in the office and the three men gathered in their usual place in the office.

Dev rang up Laxmi and asked what she was doing. She replied, "I am in the kitchen preparing some pickles. You know, I talked to Neela and she agreed to stay here during the cyclone. So I told her to go back home and get her necessary things, which she has done. What are you doing?"

"Nothing much. You know that now we have a class III warning and around five o'clock, they will upgrade it to a class IV warning. You must be very careful for the next one day. If there is anything wrong, you must phone me. I do not know if I did the right thing in taking this decision to stay in The Shop."

"Now it's too late to regret. You also be careful and do let me know every now and then as to how are you faring. Everything will be alright, think of God and do pray."

Dev asked the others if they did not want to phone their families, both said they would do it later on.

10....THE CYCLONE IS KEEPING THEM COMPANY

The three men made themselves comfortable in the office. Dev asked Kader if he had informed his mother of his whereabouts at this particular time. Kader replied, "Day before yesterday I told her that I have to be the watchman during the cyclone in a shop. She did not want to believe me at first but when I mentioned that the shop belongs to you, she voluntarily gave me the permission. And when I told her that now it is time for me to go, she gave me those Dal Puris with specific instructions that I should give them to you. I have made arrangements for her to go to her sister's place which is just a couple of doors away."

They had some tea and Dev said "Let us now review what we shall do. We are here gathered to break into the Planters Bank and remove fifty million rupees, not a cent more nor a cent less. Each of you two will get ten million rupees and I will keep the rest, that is thirty million rupees but I will not spend one cent of those thirty million. I have waited for over ten years before this project has come to this stage. I am glad that we have this cyclone and especially of this intensity.

"Of course I feel sorry for those who will suffer because of this calamity. But we have a duty to do; we shall not let anything else distract us. The bank is at a distance of one hundred yards from here. We must move when the cyclone is in the process of hitting us.

"If the cyclone's eye passes over us, we better wait for the other end of the cyclone to hit us before entering in the bank."

Around seven o'clock, the three men ate part of the food that was available and they started to unpack the tools and other equipment that will facilitate their job. First of all, Dev opened his bag. There were the string ladder, the chloroform, the dynamite sticks, the piece of string, he brought out his handkerchief, and then he had his Swiss knife, two small bottles containing some liquids and some other implements.

Michael had in his bag a number of tools that would help him to deal with the electrical side and he would switch off the electricity in the bank, be it from the supplier or from the internal generator. Of course all CCTV cameras also should be disabled before they would proceed with the job. In fact it would need to be done as soon as they entered in the bank.

Long Kader did not have much equipment for the job. He had the surgical gloves, the ladies' stockings, and he had brought three blue overalls, so that they would look all the same, and if some watchmen would see them, they would not recognize who have done the coup.

Dev said, "I have thought over our plan carefully and as I told you, I have been pondering over it for the past ten years. I have followed the career in crime of so many criminals that I have come to the inevitable conclusion that the best plans are the simplest plans. Everybody would think that this is a big bank and that the security is impregnable, that they have plenty of watchmen inside the bank, but we must remember that the security personnel also are after all human beings. They will take the risk to look after the property of their employers up to a certain extent, but generally, they would not put their lives in danger. My opinion is that violence should, at all costs, be avoided. We have children, just as the watchmen. We must think of those children before using any weapon on the watchmen. We would not like our children or the children of the watchmen to suffer because of our action. We must understand that those men are but doing their job and they are paid for it. Well, if we shall have to use violence, it must be as a last resort."

"What if we are shot at, are we entitled to shoot back, we cannot remain quiet, we may be killed or suffer severe injuries and then caught. I really do not want to go back to prison," said Kader.

"There will never be such problems in our case. Anyway, I have with me my revolver, it is charged with six bullets and I will not hesitate to use it in case of need. I will take it with me to the bank," answered Dev.

"If you have your revolver with you, Mr Dev, I have brought with me a small revolver that has been with me for quite some time." And he removed it from his sock and put it on the table. "I have already put the bullets in and it is just sort of waiting to be used."

"If you want to carry it with you, I have no objection if you will feel more secure. But please do not use it. It is dangerous. And it might land us all in prison."

"I do not have any weapon with me; I will have to rely on you to protect me. I have never stolen from a bank, or from anywhere for that matter, as we are planning to do." That was the remark made by Michael.

"Don't be unduly concerned with the security aspect; I will take care of it, provided you will look after the electricity aspect of the operation. The most important aspect of our operation will depend on the electricity aspect. You have to concentrate on that. We shall look after other things," Dev said.

Dev removed the two torchlights from the cupboard and tested them. They were working perfectly well. There was fresh news on the cyclone on radio. "We inform people that we are since the past one hour, under a Class IV cyclone warning. Members of the public are warned that the cyclone is with us. Cyclone Mady is at a distance of about twenty kilometres from the north-west coast of Cap Malheureux. On this trajectory, the cyclone will pass directly over Mauritius. Gusts of over two hundred kilometres per hour are expected. There will be very heavy rain and in several areas heavy flooding would occur. There will be flashes of lightings which will be accompanied by peals of thunder. The inhabitants are advised to stay indoors and any venture away from the houses or other places of shelter would cause untold harm to the persons themselves or to their near and dear ones. Electricity wires that would be detached from the poles could be live and nobody should touch those wires. It may be that electricity will be switched off in case of necessity. People should be ready with their candles and matches or torches in case of need." Every now and then, at an interval of about five or ten minutes, there were several flashes of lightening and peals of thunder could be heard. The sound generated by the thunder caused quite a number of buildings to shake from their foundations. At that moment, people realized that there might be casualties in the country.

Many persons, even those who normally do not pray, made some silent prayers. So Dev thought that all persons pray when they feel that they will be the loser in a calamity, but tomorrow they will forget about the prayer and go about their business as if nothing has occurred.

The newscaster continued with the advice. Dev was thinking how many persons pay heed to the good advice given by the authorities. Outside, the wind speed was visibly increasing, rain was falling as never before. People could not sleep, not even the children who were scared as to what would happen to them. The parents tried to comfort them, but to no avail, as the parents themselves were as scared as the children.

There was a cyclone crisis cell that was meeting at the Line Barracks with the higher rank Police Officers. The officers were told that this cyclone was stronger than any cyclone that they have witnessed. They will have to do their best to protect the life and property of our people. "There will be many calls for assistance from members of the public. I would advise the superintendents responsible for their districts to use their best judgments as to what should be done in the circumstances. Gentlemen, good luck to you," said the Commissioner of Police. When the members had left, the Commissioner murmured one of his prayers that he used to say every day.

At about ten o'clock, the cyclone was at its strongest. Dev thought that he would ring up his wife for a last time…that day. Laxmi picked up the phone after the first ringing and Dev asked her how it was that she was so quick to pick up the phone when otherwise she takes her time?

Laxmi asked him, "How are you? I hope you have not been unduly affected by what we are going through."

"I am alright, so is Michael. Another person whom I have known since he was a child is here to keep us company. We have had our food, we shall drink the tea which you had prepared for us. Neela is with you I take it."

"Yes, but you be careful. I am scared for you. Be careful." Laxmi was really worried for him, but he has to perform his duty, she thought.

Dev told his companions that he had decided to rest for some time, "We still have about four hours before we start for our duty. But before doing that, ring up your families, otherwise they might try to ring you up. They took their rest in the sitting position in which they found themselves. Dev walked about the room. He was not feeling sleepy. His mind was occupied and when your mind is occupied, you don't feel sleepy and if you do, you don't get a full sleep, as if you your eyes get closed but immediately get reopened. Dev was thinking whether what he was doing could ever be justified? What he had endured could not be told now. For him it was not a question of money. It was a matter of honour. But what if he failed in his endeavor? What if he got caught? But then it was not the time to think of what he was about to do. He had taken upon himself the task to teach those people a lesson. So be it. He would go ahead; the only problem would be his responsibility for his companions. They had a blind trust in him, he could not let them down at this juncture, and he hoped that there would be no casualty. Dev was thinking of casualties from the operation he would conduct, at the same time, he was thinking of casualties in the wider context, from the effects of cyclone Mady.

Around one o'clock, the three were up. They had some tea and some cakes. All of a sudden, it was dark. If you have ever been in the dark when a cyclone is at its peak, you must have felt that the final moment has come. The three companions were very quiet for some time until Dev said,

"Can either of you get the torches? They are near to you Michael." The torch lighted the room. Then they switched the generator and there was light again.

The radio was on; talk was going on with news and views about the cyclone. "Many places, half of Mauritius I would say, are deprived of electricity. Many electricity poles have been blown down. We cannot continue supplying electricity in the affected areas. In the circumstances we have to interrupt supply in those areas. And this has been done to ensure the safety of our people. In about an hour's time, the cyclone's eye will pass over Mauritius. At that time, the weather will be very calm, because, as you know, there is no cyclonic activity in the middle of the cyclone. The eye will take some time to go through the country, depending on the speed of the cyclone and the diameter of the eye. We are making a special appeal to people that they should not venture out of where they are. The second part of the cyclone that will pass over the country is much more dangerous than the first part. This can be explained very simply. This will be done later. The buildings that are not strong enough and the trees that have been their shaken in their roots by the first part of the cyclone will be blown down easily. We appeal to all Mauritians to stay indoors." And the news continued interrupted by some songs.

Around ten o'clock, the cyclone started calming down and in about an hour, it was completely calm. Dev and his two companions opened the door of the shop and had a look outside. There was no electricity and so no lights. Everything seemed to be so quiet and so calm, and at the same time so oppressive, so eerie, as if pressing them down. Michael brought the torch with him, he lighted it and had a look in the direction of the bank, but he could not see anybody in the street. He walked a few yards and noticed that a slight rain had started falling, but there was nothing more. There were some branches that were lying in the street as well as a few iron sheets normally used to cover the roofs of buildings. But these days, there were very few buildings covered with iron sheets, most were in concrete. In the 1960's, when there were quite a number of rather strong cyclones, most of the wooden houses covered with iron sheets or covered with thatch were blown down and since then all buildings that had been constructed were in reinforced concrete. So in a cyclone, very few houses are damaged in their structure. Of course, the people have Nature to contend with, with the wind and the rain mainly.

They then entered the shop and Dev said, "It is nearly time to start on our mission." The radio was continuing to broadcast news about the cyclone. The newscaster was saying, "The calm is deceptive, the part of the cyclone that will follow would be more violent than the first part. People must not go outside. We have been informed that on the side of Rose Hill, a few persons are walking in the streets. What they are doing is most dangerous. They are called upon to go back to and in their homes or in the shelters. We have been informed that four persons have lost their lives. Two from drowning, one while trying to cross an overflowing canal and one in the harbor. One met an accident when he touched a live electricity wire that was detached from its pole and the fourth one died after he was hit be flying iron sheets that had been detached from the roof of a building".

They sat down waiting for the cyclone to start again with the gusts of wind blowing from the contrary direction to the earlier part of the cyclone. Time appeared to have come to a stop, contrary to flitting as usual; it was stationary as if it has forgotten to move. You must have remarked that for the good things of life, Time travels not only fast, but very fast, but when you are going through trying times, time stays still for a long time, as if to make you suffer the longest time possible. Such is the behavior of time towards us. But we have to put up with this type of behavior. Nature so wills it.

Dev and his companions were not in the mood to engage in any sort of conversation. They checked and rechecked their tools and other equipment.

After a calm of about four hours, the cyclone started waking up. The wind started blowing, slowly at first then gathering momentum. Rain started falling, again slowly, and then it started falling in a torrent. Lightening was playing in the sky and the peals of thunder were like huge cannons going off. All told, this part of the cyclone was, or at least gave the feeling that it was, far more violent than the first part.

Dev said, "In five minutes time, we make a move. I wish and pray that we shall succeed in our endeavor. Let us pray, each according to our respective belief." And he prayed silently. So did Michael as well as Kader. They collected their tools and they put on the overalls. They put a stocking over their head and face. Dev put his revolver in the pocket of his overall, and three nylon bags which he collected from the cupboard went into his bag.

Dev said "Whatever happens, do not panic. Now let us go to face our great adventure." He opened the main door they went out and he locked the door again.

11....MISSION SUCCESSFULLY COMPLETED

When Dev, Michael and Kader were in the street, they found that it was difficult to keep their balance. The wind was blowing so fiercely that they felt that they would be blown away with the next gust. It was impossible for them to walk side by side; it was better that they be one behind the other. Flashes of lightening were lighting the sky and everything else and they could see ahead of them that there was nothing and nobody moving. Rain was sending the message that it is not going to relent for a long time. In such circumstances the three adventurers were in the street.

Moving very slowly, the three were making a very difficult progress towards the Planters Bank. Kader was nearly swept away by the combined effect of the wind and rain, but at the last moment he was caught by Dev and Michael. Somehow they managed to be near the main door of the Bank. Here they went in a corner and Dev told them that he will have to use dynamite sticks to open the door. It was pitch dark, and Michael used his torch in order to get some light. Dev took out two sticks of dynamite from his bag. He used some tape to stick them to the front of the door. After two minutes, the dynamite was ready to be fired. Dev knew that in about twelve seconds, the dynamite sticks would blow up part of the door from the time that fire is set to the sticks. But he must time the firing in such a manner that it would coincide with noise of the thunder. The noise created by the dynamite must join the noise of the thunder. Both noises will be one in such a way that those who will hear it will conclude that the thunder is getting louder.

Dev had to wait for about thirty seconds when there was flash of lightening, the whole sky seemed to be lighted. There were not only flashes, but rather a series of flashes. Dev was ready to set fire to the dynamite, he did it and in ten seconds, peals of thunder started to create a very loud noise. This loud noise was mixed with the noise of the blowing up of the door by the double sticks of dynamite.

The door was damaged, the three persons could get access in the bank. There was no electricity in the bank except that provided by the private generator. Dev and his friends stopped behind a big column in the bank. They tried to detect some movement of the watchmen, but there was no movement. They could see that there was light in the basement.

Quietly, Michael opened his bag and took out some tools like pliers and was ready to disable the CCTV. He knew where the wires were but he wanted to cut the electricity supply at source. Dev opened his bag and took out a metal container and poured the liquid from the container onto his handkerchief. He put the handkerchief in his pocket. He then signaled to Kader for his handkerchief and he did the same with that as well. He then signaled them to move in the basement. When they were half way down the stairs, they could see clearly the two watchmen sitting on easy chairs. One was sleeping but the other was wide awake.

Both Dev and Kader had their handkerchiefs which contained a heavy dose of chloroform ready. Dev took his revolver in his right hand and slowly the three companions moved towards the watchmen. The one who was awake was surprised to see the three and was about to wake up his friend when Dev pointed his pistol towards him and slowly told him that he should not make any noise otherwise his revolver will fire six shots.

"Just raise your hands and you will come to no harm," he said.

By then, the other watchman was awake. He looked surprised. Dev continued "You will come to no harm, we are not interested in your life and we have no intention to harm you. Just keep quiet. We have to tie you up and we ask you not to put up any resistance. He moved to one of the watchmen and applied his chloroform containing handkerchief to his nose and mouth and Kader did the same to the other watchman. Both watchmen went to sleep for at least four hours, so said Kader.

Michael moved away from the two and he went towards the other part of the basement and in five minutes, there was no electricity at all in the bank. It simply meant that the electricity generator had been disabled. Dev took the piece of rope that he had brought and cut it in two pieces. He gave one piece to Kader and he used the other piece to tie the hands and feet of the watchmen. This done, they went towards the strong room and the vault. On the right side was the private safes area, meant for the clients and on the left was the strong room. Dev told his companions to move to the other corner and he took two sticks of dynamite got them together with a piece of tape and placing them in a specific place in the corner, he lighted the fuse. There was a loud noise. They could now enter the strong room and had access to the safe itself, because this was where the money was kept.

Dev was working alone, his companions were just watching him. Dev knew that to get into the safe more intelligence must be used than force. It was the same as getting into the strong room. The doors of modern day bank safes cannot be forced. Maybe you need two different keys. Maybe you need a special code to open the door, the scientists have devised other methods to discourage those who pick all types of safes. Most thieves concentrate on opening the door of the safes. But they fail to take into consideration the other parts of the safes. And this is where Dev concentrated his intelligence and his efforts.

He preferred to enter the safe through the flank. There was a small-sized container in which there was a bluish liquid. He also had a smaller bottle in which there was a rose-coloured liquid. The stopper of this bottle was made of glass and not of cork. The others knew that this was the dangerous liquid.

The first liquid was poured by the side of the safe, about two tea spoonful, then about half a tea spoonful of the other liquid was very slowly poured on the first liquid. Immediately it was noticed that there was a thick smoke emanating from where the two liquids met. Slowly and slowly, Dev worked round a whole through which a man can get into the safe. He sent the two others to see if the two watchmen were still fast asleep, and in a minute they confirmed that they were still fast asleep. In fifteen minutes a hole through Dev which could enter in the safe was created.

Dev took out from his bag the three plastic bags that he had brought with him. He went inside the safe and told the two others to wait for him and he would pass on the money. They would have to put it in the bags. He was gone for about five minutes. Then his hand appeared. It was holding a bundle of bank notes and went inside and came with several bundles which were placed in the bags. Dev brought in all fifty bundles, then came out of the safe. All three bags were more or less half full.

They had a proper look out to find out if they had collected all the tools and other implements they had come with, and each picking one bag, as well as their personal bag, they started to move out. When they were passing by the two watchmen, Dev said that he will release one of them and he can free the other. But then he said that they did not want to leave the other bit of rope also behind. He had his Swiss knife with him and both watchmen were freed and the strings was put in the bag of Dev. There was no light but the torch was giving enough light to let them do what they were doing.

They went upstairs and the torches were switched off but then it was impossible for them to move out. One torch was kept lighted. The cyclone was as strong as when they had entered the bank. When they came near the door, the torch was put off and they depended on the lightening to provide them guidance. Soon they were near the street. They were walking very close to the wall of the building and then they saw a light. They did not know what to do. Dev told the two others that they must not move, to be part of the décor. Then whoever will pass near to them will not know that any other person is around. In fact two persons went by them, talking in a loud voice. One of them was saying "I am sure that there will not be anybody in the Bank in this cyclonic weather. We shall remove as much money as possible and then we shall not have to work to earn our livelihood."

The other replied, "Let us hope that really there will not be any watchman…" And by then they had passed Dev and his companions. These latter started to go back to The Shop and the crossed the street and ten minutes after, Dev opened the main door and they were in The Shop. The door was locked, they went in the office.

They removed the gloves, the stocking from their face and head, as well as the overalls. Then Dev told them that the first thing they must do is to dispose of everything disposable because "nothing that was used for the coup should be traced to us. Let us put everything that we must get rid of into a plastic bag and we shall see how to dispose of it."

Nobody was talking of the coup or of the money. Dev started to talk about what they had done. He said, "Our endeavor has been successful, thanks to the close cooperation of all three of us. Let us see what we have in the bags.

The money was taken out of the bags and they placed the bundles on the table. They had ten stacks of five bundles each. "As we had decided, each of you will receive ten million. Each of you is entitled to take your ten bundles and they are all yours. I have thirty million for me, and I remember having told you that I will not spend a cent of that money. Maybe someday you will know why I planned and executed this coup."

Both Michael and Long Kader were still quiet but at last Michael said, "Mr Dev, I have a greater respect for you now. I knew that I could rely on the success of our job, but still I had some doubt in my innermost mind. I am thankful to you."

And Kader added "I have always known you. I have not had a secondary school education but I have always trusted you and I have a blind faith in your capacity."

"Each one can take his share. However, I would like to say something to you. People get caught when they misuse what comes in their grip. I know many persons who have regretted their action not because of a coup in which they participated, but because they changed their lifestyle. I have already told you about this.

"If you want to take what belongs to you I have no objection. You are free to take my advice or to reject it. I have a dream for each of you. Kader, I know that the land on which you have your house belongs to your mother. The house is not worth anything, it is time to pull it down and have a new construction. You can have a shop in front and the residential part will be in the rear.

"You have some experience in buying and selling and it will not be difficult for you to manage your own shop. For your building you can get a loan on the guarantee of the land, of course you will not need the loan, but your neighbours, friends and relatives will start putting questions about you and on the source of your finance. The loan is a good idea.

"Michael, you also can think of a good house and you also can look for a portion of land on which there is an old building that has remained unoccupied for a long time. Get a loan to buy the land and use the land as a guarantee, the loan and the purchase can be arranged in a single transaction. You can use the land as a second guarantee to get a further loan to construct a building, residential as well as commercial. You can use the front part of the building as an office or to do some trade. You were telling me that your wife would like to prepare cakes that you will place with the vendors. Here is an opportunity that you cannot miss.

"Think carefully about what I have said. If you want, I can keep your money in my safe here. You can take them right now or let it lie here until needed. That is, if you trust me."

Both Michael and Kader protested that doubted the trust they had in him. Kader was the first to say that he agreed to the suggestion of Dev. He said "I know that you will never think of causing any loss to me. I have always needed someone like you to guide me. I will follow the advice that you are giving me. Let the money be kept by you until I will need it. I know that I will take the money little by little and that also when needed. Keep the money with you, Mr Dev. That is all I will say."

And Michael could not be behind Kader. He said, "You know about my good for nothing son-in-law. If he would come to know that I have some money, he will make the life of my daughter hell. He will try to lay his hands on whatever money that I will have with me. If you can keep my share with you, I will be grateful to you. I agree with what you are proposing. I do not think that I shall start spending whatever I shall get so soon. I shall do what you are proposing."

Both Michael and Kader were wondering where the fifty million rupees could be kept. Dev guessed what they were thinking. He said "You did not realize how much money fifty million rupees would be. I am not talking about the value. Because you know that fifty million is fifty million. I am talking about the physical space that fifty million rupees in notes would occupy. Even if the notes are in denomination of a thousand rupee. I will tell you to be careful as to how you will start spending your money."

Dev decided to keep the money that they had removed from the bank in a more secure place. The wood panelling on one side of the wall of the office was in fact a concealed door. Dev opened it to disclose a safe six feet tall and about four feet in width. He brought two keys and with them he opened the door of the safe. What the two companions could see in the safe was a stack of papers and a small box. They brought all their money and put them in the safe. Dev got two sheets and wrote down

"For Kader ……Rs.10,000,000"
"For Michael…..Rs.10,000,000"

And he locked the safe and the wooden panel as well. They then had some cakes and some soft drinks. They cleaned the room to get rid of any telltale matter.

Dev asked Kader if he would need the overalls, he said "I think Michael would put them to better use. But before using them, he must give them a good wash."

Michael thanked him and said "I can use them for my work. They will give me a more professional air." So he packed the overalls in one of the bags which he put aside. They did not know what to do with the stockings and therefore it was decided that they should be destroyed, as well as the gloves and the pieces of rope. The chloroform as well as the other liquids could not just be thrown away. Kader was asked to throw the chloroform in a canal where there was running water and Dev kept the other liquids in his bag. Dev said that it would be easier for Kader to dispose of the pieces of rope and the gloves, so he instructed him to dirty them in the mud and throw them in a municipality bin. "You should follow these instructions to the letter in order to be on the safe side."

It was about four thirty in the morning and soon it will be morning. They decided to take some rest. But they did not feel like taking a rest because their minds were occupied on matters that would not allow them to rest. The cyclone was not as violent as it was two or three hours ago. Dev put the light on in the shop and he checked the openings. His shop had not suffered from the adverse effects of the cyclone, thank God he thought.

The radio was on and they could follow the progress of the cyclone. According to the latest piece of news, ten persons had lost their lives. There was untold destruction all over the place. All the canals, rivulets and rivers had overflowed their banks, all reservoirs were full, and about twenty five per cent of the houses had suffered serious damage, if not were completely blown down. Even some government buildings had suffered from the cyclone. There were some cases of pilferage even during the middle of the cyclone. No mention was made of a theft in one of the banks. Around five o'clock,

Dev opened the front door of his shop to have a look at what was happening outside. He stepped on the pavement and looked on the right, then on the left. Water a foot deep was running in the street. There were iron sheets that had been blocked by some columns and some columns had fallen and the telephone and electricity wires were lying on the road and on the pavement. And there were small branches and leaved strewn everywhere. The two friends of Dev had joined him on the pavement. They wondered how was it possible for them to come out in the very violent cyclonic weather and at night time. "If it would have been during day time, I would never have dared to venture out, but at night everything goes. Especially when we are guided by a leader of the calibre of Mr Dev," said Kader.

They went inside and listened to the radio. After a song, an announcement was made. "Cyclone Mady has started moving away from Mauritius. However the class IV warning is maintained until further notice. People are strongly advised to stay indoors. It is very dangerous to walk on the streets, especially as live electricity wires maybe lying on the ground and they represent a deadly trap. Seventy five percent of the electricity supply has been switched off, and only twenty five per cent of supply has been maintained in some specific areas. We advise people not to venture out. We shall issue a further bulletin in an hour's time."

Dev rang up Laxmi and again she picked up the phone immediately. "How are you? You did not suffer too much in the cyclone?" Dev asked her.

"It was very frightening, especially you away from home. How are you?"

"I am alright. I agree with you that the cyclone was frightening; we could not sleep, let alone have a rest. You must pray to God that there has been no serious incident affecting our close ones."

Laxmi said "When can you come home?"

"The cyclone warning is still in force, but I am more or less sure that it will be lifted in the next one hour. But then we must be sure that the roads have not been damaged. Let us hope that fallen trees have not blocked the main road to Vacoas. Anyway, I shall be seeing you soon. Be careful and I am telling you not to go out of the house."

Michael also rang up his family and he was told that part of their house had to be abandoned because some window panes were broken by a flying sheet of iron and also some branches had been responsible for causing further damage, but all told, they were alright. He told them that he would come as soon as the roads would be open. Kader did not want to telephone because he knew that his mother was at the house of his aunt – that is the sister of his mother.

Around six thirty, there was a further broadcast about the cyclone. "There is in no cyclone warning in force in Mauritius as from six o'clock this morning. The authorities have decided to lift all cyclone warnings. Cyclone Mady has left our shores and it is now situated at a distance of about forty kilometres from the south-south-west coast and it is moving at a speed of about nine kilometres per hour. Gusts of wind would be felt for some hours still and rain will continue falling for another five or six hours, though it will not be falling in torrents. People are strongly advised to be careful when stepping out of their houses or other shelters. They should not come in contact or touch electricity wires that have been detached from the columns, they may be live.

"We have been informed that ten persons have lost their lives due to the effects of the cyclone. We would also advise members of the public not to go near the rivers and canals because the volume of water is far greater than is witnessed in a normal cyclone.

"Most of the roads cannot be used by motor traffic. Some of them have been damaged by the rain but the main problem is because of the fact that trees have fallen on the roads and unless the trees are removed from the streets, we would not advise motorists to venture in those streets. The motorways have not been damaged and they are open to circulation but the roads in the villages, the towns and the city cannot be used."

Some more news of the cyclone was given and at the end there came the announcement that the Prime Minister would address the people at eight o'clock.

Dev told Kader that he had not had any news of his mother; he would do better to go to his place and talk to his mother. "I know how parents feel about their children, however grown up they may be. I am sure she must be worried about you and now that the cyclone is almost gone, you must be home."

Kader said, "I was thinking of the same thing. So if both of you have no objection, I would go home and give some consolation to my mother and I would like to know how my house has managed in the cyclone. I will see you maybe tomorrow."

He went into the shop, collected his effects as well as the bag containing the things that have to be deposed of in the municipal bin and in the canal and went to his house. Dev told Michael, "We also must make a move. I am worried and I would like to reach home soon. Let us take our effects and go to the car. The shop was closed and they walked rather slowly to the car. It was easy to drive to the Hong Kong Bank and also to the State Commercial Bank. But then after that there was about three feet deep of water from the sea. The sea had breached its bank. He made a U-turn and took the next street which led him to Government House and to what is called the Chaussee Street. Then he went through Moka Street, by the Line Barracks Police Station until he arrived to the Maupin Street Junction. He turned into Maupin Street which led him to the motorway. Some of the buildings along Moka Street were heavily damaged, some had lost their roof and most of the separations which were made with corrugated iron sheets had fallen down as if there had never any separation between the houses. Many persons were standing in small groups and evidently they were talking of the effects of the cyclone. About a hundred persons were gathered near the police station of Line Barracks.

So far, Dev was driving very carefully and at a slow speed. When he reached the motorway, he saw a few cars that were coming down. He signaled for one car to stop and the other driver obliged. Dev just asked him if the road was not damaged or blocked from where he was coming. He was told that the motorway was alright, but in the inhabited areas, many roads cannot be used as they have been blocked by fallen trees.

He asked Dev "where do you have to go?"

"I am bound for Vacoas. And where are you going?"

"I am coming from Curepipe and I will try to go to Triolet. All my relatives are there, I haven't had news about them, so I consider it my duty to find out how they have managed in the cyclone. Well, I say good luck to you."

Dev then started driving his car with more confidence and in half an hour's time, he was on the St Paul Road near Phoenix. He was going on the main road because the risk of risk of fallen trees across that road was less than in the side roads.

He then went to the traffic lights and then he turned onto street where he lived. But soon he came to a place where the road was completely blocked by tree trunks. He had to turn back and take another road and try to reach his place in a round-about way. He saw municipal workers who were busy trying to clear and free at least half of the width of the roads. And they were helped by the inhabitants of the area.

Dev had to leave his car at a distance of about two hundred and fifty yards from his home because there was no possibility to drive up to his place. He took his bag and Michael did the same with his. Michael had another plastic bag. They walked to the house of Dev, Michael continued further up and Dev entered in his house. The door was not locked.

Laxmi was in the kitchen, preparing their lunch. Dev looked at her, his eyes moist, without saying anything. Laxmi also looked at him, then Dev saw that she was weeping, rather sobbing. Not loudly, but quietly and Dev could not hold back his tears. His tears also started flowing. He held her in his arms and for about two minutes they were like that.

At last Dev said, "Never again you will have to undergo such a situation." Laxmi simply added, "Let me prepare some tea. I also haven't had mine, neither has Neela. You must be hungry; I will get something to eat." She prepared three mugs of tea, the third was for Neela. Neela entered the kitchen. "How are you Neela. I hope that you did not suffer too much in the cyclone. I take it that your house has not been damaged."

Neela told him, "I do not know, I haven't been to see my house yet."

Laxmi added, "Neela has been keeping me company. She has not had time to go her place yet, especially that she does not know whether the streets are open."

"I can understand that. I have left my car near the cinema hall because there is no way to bring it up to our house. When you go to your place Neela, you must not touch nor come into contact with the electric wires. Be very careful. Laxmi, why don't we walk Neela to her place? You can see for yourself what damage the cyclone has caused around here."

Laxmi said, "In about half an hour. I have rice and curry on the cooking unit, I cannot move now."

Neela told her, "Madam, finish with your cooking. In the meantime, I will finish what I am doing. Then we can go together."

Laxmi put enough rice and curries for Neela in a container that would be enough for her lunch as well as dinner.

At nine o'clock, the Prime Minister was on the radio as well as on television. He said "Ladies and Gentlemen, the country and all of us have gone through, and are still going through, traumatizing moments with cyclone Mady. We have not had to face a cyclone of the strength and intensity of Mady in a very long time.

"We are sorry to know that ten persons have lost their lives, from one cause or another, but we feel that even one death is too many. We sympathize with the relatives and friends who are affected by the passing away of these Mauritians.

"About eighty to ninety percent of our agricultural produce has been destroyed. We can say that all our vegetable plantation has been destroyed. We can say the same thing in so far as our fruits are concerned. We shall depend a hundred per cent on importation of all vegetables and fruits for the next three to six months. We are grateful that we shall have the help of our traditionally friendly countries.

"Seventy five percent of the electricity supply has had to be interrupted and this has been done keeping in mind the safety of the people. The Central Electricity Board employees are already busy repairing the faulty and damaged lines. I would request our citizens to exercise some patience and leave the CEB workers to do their job. I am informed that at least two friendly countries have decided to help us. They are sending teams of three hundred and two hundred technicians respectively, who will work with the employees of the CEB to restore electricity at the earliest moment.

"Roads have been blocked by fallen trees and other material from the damaged houses. The employees of the Ministry of Works, with the help of other employees from other ministries, are trying to free the roads. Here I must say that we cannot forget the help of the Engineer Corps of the Special Support Unit of the Police Force, which is out in the streets with all the necessary equipment and the members are providing us with a special service in helping to clear our streets.

"In view of the damages suffered in the country, government has decided that all schools, secondary and primary as well as the universities will be closed for one week.

"We have received reports of criminal activities during the cyclone. The most daring one has been a hold-up in the Planters Bank. One of the persons involved lost his life when he was shot by a watchman. One managed to escape but a third has been captured and now is in Police custody. Some other cases of theft have also been reported and the police are enquiring into those cases."

"The Central Water Authority has started verifying our water supply and bringing corrective measures wherever needed, but people must wait for the electricity to pump the water in quite a number of cases.

"In these difficult times, government will do everything possible to make the life of the people as easy as is humanly possible. It is in a time like the one we are going through presently that we must think how we can help our friends and Mauritians are very good at helping their friends and neighbours."

And the Prime Minister continued on the same line for some time.

After one hour, Dev and Laxmi left home to accompany Neela and the desolation was painful to see. It looked as if the cyclone had deliberately wrought havoc simply to make people suffer. Electrical wires were lying on the ground. Dev told them "it is a good idea that electricity has been switched off. Before electricity will be switched on, all the electricity lines and all the columns have to be checked and verified. And this will take some time to do, maybe one month or more. Let us hope that some of the friendly countries that are helping us are conversant with what is to be done and the electricity will be part of us again. We can also expect them to help in constructing some houses in the country."

When they arrived where Neela was living, all of them went inside. Water had seeped in the house. Some window panes had been broken and that also contributed with more water in the house. The curtains were wet and it would take some time to put order in the house.

Dev asked her, "Do you know somebody to replace the broken glass panes?"

She answered, "No sir, I must look for somebody to do it." Dev was thinking that he also has to replace some window panes. He told her that if he will meet someone who does the job, he will send him to her place.

Laxmi told her that if she feels like, she can come and stay at their place until the window panes are replaced. Then they moved out. They passed through some other streets where they saw groups of workers busy clearing the streets. Some of the workers knew Dev and they greeted him. Part of the road leading to his place was cleared and in about an hour, he would be able to drive his car right up to his house. He told Laxmi, "Let us take the car and we can drive to the main road, and see if the supermarkets and the other shops are open. You can do some shopping."

The supermarkets and the shops were open, they purchased some items, especially, that those that would become scarce after the cyclone. Then they went to the place where they sold glass panes of all sizes and variety. Dev knew the owner and he told him that four glass panes at his place had to be replaced and also five panes at the place of another person. The owner of the place said, "I have two assistants who can go to your place in the van. There will be panes of different sizes and they can cut them to the required size if needed. They can go right now, or it can be done tomorrow. What do you say?"

Dev replied, "Let them come now. Then I will take them to the other place."

"I know where you live, but the assistants don't." He called his assistants and told them what they should do. Dev arrived at his place and in half an hour, the broken panes were replaced. Then Dev and Laxmi went to the place of Neela and the assistants followed them in their van. At Neela's place, the job was completed in about forty five minutes. Dev wanted to pay them for the glass panes and for the work. But the assistants told him that he must effect payment to their boss in the shop. But he did not fail to give them a good tip. He then went to pay the owner of the shop selling the panes whatever he owed him.

He told Laxmi that he had something else to do. He drove towards the place of Michael and he was at home. He came near the car and Dev asked him how he was doing, how were his relatives and whether the house had suffered from severe damages. Dev was assured that everything was under control. Then Dev said, "I need a generator, the same type that you installed in the shop. I will be grateful if you can do it as soon as possible."

Michael was quick to respond, "When will you buy it? I can start work on it tomorrow if you wish. You must get a mason first. Let him complete the structure to house the generator."

Dev said "There is no need to for that. My dog house is not being used since my dog died. We can house the generator there. All we need is a metallic door. This can be arranged. If you are free tomorrow, you can have a look and then we can go to the shop and buy the generator. Do you think that we can carry the generator in the boot of my car?"

"I think you can. I will come to your place at around eight o'clock tomorrow morning."

"How did you pass the time of the cyclone? I have a feeling that your family did not suffer too much." Laxmi asked Michael.

"We were a bit scared in The Shop but things turned out to be alright, Madam. My family is alright. My wife is preparing food, if you feel like having some, you are welcome." Laxmi thanked him and said that they will have to go home.

It was near to noon and Dev told Laxmi, "Now I will have my lunch and then I am going to have a nice sleep. What would you do?"

"I'll do the same. I am feeling very sleepy you know. I did not sleep at all last night. It's time to catch up."

So they had their lunch but then came along the sister and the brother in law of Laxmi. They are very nice people and they were at Dev's place to find out how they had fared during the cyclone. And if they needed any help. Laxmi told her sister Renu that Dev was not at home during the cyclone but at The Shop.

Dev told them, "I had to be in the shop, but I was not alone. The electrician, Michael was with me and so was another person I know from Port Louis. The night was frightful, I can tell you that much. Laxmi was in the company of Neela, I can envisage how difficult it must have been for her to stay in the house when the window panes were broken in the cyclone."

Laxmi's brother in law, Sunil, said, "Thank God we are all safe. But Laxmi could have come to our place before the cyclone."

Dev said, "Sunil, I will be installing a generator for home use, in case we would have another cyclone. I have already installed one in the shop and you know its importance only when you are deprived of electricity. Anyway, tomorrow the electrician will be here around five o'clock and if you want to have a look, do drop in."

Sunil, for that is his name, responded, "I can come tomorrow. Now I will try to go to Riviere du Rempart. I have not received any news from my relatives but I don't know whether the road is clear or not. I'll just try and see how far I can reach."

Then both Dev and Laxmi had a nice sleep and they woke up around six o'clock. They had tea and some cakes that they had bought when they had been out earlier, after which they visited some friends and also two relatives.

PART III - AFTERMATH

12.....THE EFFECTS OF THE CYCLONE

The following day, Dev went to the shop a little bit earlier than usual. Most of the stores were not open for transacting business, but they were open for cleaning purposes. Anyway, there were no clients. The effects of the cyclone were very much visible. The workers in the various shops were cleaning the pavement in front of their respective premises. As soon as they saw Dev, they put him a hundred questions, which he answered to the best of his ability in the circumstances. He asked them how they fared in the cyclone; they informed him that there was no problem for some of them. Others had lost their property, their houses and other effects. Now the houses that are still standing have got to be cleaned and the clothing have to be dried. This can only be done when the weather will turn sunny.

When Dev was entering The Shop, one of his employees asked him, "Have you heard of the crime in the Planters Bank, where one person has been killed and the safe of the bank has been forced open?"

Dev said, "I have heard of it on the radio. It appears that one of the criminals has been arrested, one was killed and one has escaped. How much money have they stolen from the bank, have you heard something about this?"

"I have not been told about the sum that has been stolen, but it appears that the robbers stole more than twenty five million rupees."

Dev had to wait patiently for the newspapers to get the news of the outcome of the cyclone. He sent his messenger to the Central Market to find out if the papers were out and if so, to get to get a copy of each of them. Only one paper was out and the messenger brought it and Dev started reading it immediately. There were lots of photos of the damages caused by the cyclone and there were some pictures of the Planters Bank and of the main door that looked heavily damaged. Then there were pictures of the inside of the bank, the staircase leading to the strong room and to the vault. The strong room as well as the vault with the damages to them were also shown but people thought that those damages were not that heavy.

The dead person has been taken to the hospital for autopsy purposes after the forensic officers and the doctor had completed their job on the scene of the crime. Many of the Police Officers were busy trying to get some finger prints of the criminals and of others.

The alleged criminal was in Police custody and the Police Officers of the Central Criminal Investigation Department, otherwise known as the CCID, were already busy with him, to get the name and address of his alleged accomplice who had escaped. The two watchmen were being interrogated by different officers, and in their case, the Police were trying to find out whether they were accomplices in the crime. The officers of the bank gave a first estimate that the bank may have lost about fifty five million rupees.

Dev then read about the damages of the cyclone. There were human casualties and that was very telling that people have scant regard for warnings of dangers, at least in the majority of cases. The cyclone refugee centres were full in certain areas, government had to provide those refugees a sum of money on a daily basis, to each person in the centres, plus some bread, biscuits, bottled water and other things. In some areas there were no refugees, in others there were some, who were genuine refugees, in still others, there were many supposed refugees. They came to those centres with the intention of not leaving those places, they wanted to get a house from the government, of course without paying and all sorts of benefit. Trying to get some work, earn some money, looking after their family is not in their culture, they prefer to be dependents of anybody they can find willing to help them.

Some buildings used both as residences and for commercial and industrial purposes were blown down, many others were damaged but still in a repairable state. Crops were more or less totally destroyed. Some water mains were clogged with mud and had to be cleaned. Above all, seventy five per cent of the electricity supply was switched off, which left a majority of the population in complete darkness. In these periods you really feel that you must have done something wrong or against the established order of Nature to deserve such a Fate.

After some time, Michael came in the shop. He talked to the employees of The Shop and told them that he was with Dev during the cyclone as well as Long Kader and how difficult it was to pass the night. Then he went to see Dev. They talked again about the effects of the cyclone and Dev asked him if he was ready to go and buy the generator, of the same brand and of the same capacity as the one he has installed in the Shop. "You can come to my place maybe about four of five o'clock and start your work. A brother-in-law of mine, Sunil, you must know him, might come to see how the work is being done and he also might then like to install the same type of generator at his place."

They went to purchase the generator and told the salesman that they would collect it at about four the same afternoon. They then went in The Shop. Dev asked his messenger to get some Dal Puris for lunch and he added "Get us some 'Gateaux Piments and some Alouda' as well. See to it that the Alouda is not contaminated…no, I would prefer some freshly made tea, I do not want to take the risk of having stomach troubles in addition to the other troubles we have."

When they were having their lunch, Kader came and he shared some lunch as well. Dev asked him how was his mother? He replied, "My mother is not bad healthwise, but we have lost our house. Thank God that she was at her sister's place. Now we have no house at all, I do not know what to do.

I have come to see you to get some advice. What should I do in the immediate future?"

Dev asked him "Can your aunt put up with your mother for about a month? You must propose this to your aunt and tell her that you will pay a certain sum of money for her trouble."

"I can do that. I had kept ten thousand rupees at home in a small box. I found the box in the rubbles and the rubbish," and he showed them the money that had been tied in a dirty handkerchief.

"Are you ready to construct a new house? Your mother has the land, and you must get a loan."

"Who will give me a loan?"

"Let your mother apply for the loan. She will give the land and the still unconstructed building as collateral for the loan. You will stand as the guarantor and I am sure that you can get your loan."

"Where shall I start? I am asking you about this because I do not know what demarches I have to make."

"First of all, talk to your mother. Get her to agree about the building. If she agrees, you must clear the land of all the rubbish lying on it, then you must get a plan of the building made. You can start looking for people to help you clear the site, you can put up a small lean-to in a corner where you will live as a watchman and help in the construction. You must come and see me around two o'clock tomorrow. I will take you to a person working at the municipality who will help you with the plan. You must bring the title deed and a plan of the land. I suppose you have them?"

"All the papers have been lost. I do not know what to do." His eyes became moist and he was about to start crying.

"We then shall have to do something about it. But do come here tomorrow at two o'clock."

Michael said that he would have to buy what he needed for the installation of the generator and he accompanied Kader out of the shop. After a few minutes, Dev wanted to have a walk to the Central Market and the area where the Planters Bank is situated. Other newspapers were already out and he bought a copy of each of them. He went by the Planters Bank and he saw workers who were busy repairing the damaged door. Some persons were just standing around and talking and watching. He also stood by for a few minutes and tried to pay attention to what people were saying. He heard someone saying that it was a very daring robbery, and another saying that the person arrested could not have done it. A third one said that it must have been an insider job, and the watchmen must be accomplices. So was the opinion of a section of the public.

Dev arrived at The Shop and by then it was nearly four o'clock. He was talking to the employees and Dev told them that he must pick up the generator and go home. One of the employees told him "You are having a generator installed at home, but is it not a bit late? You should have done it last week."

"If only I had known that we shall have to face such a cyclone, I would of course have installed the generator last week, but unfortunately, I cannot as yet read the mind of God. Or can I?"

At home, Dev and Michael could not get the generator from the boot of the car, they had to get the help of some other person. By then, Laxmi prepared some tea. Michael saw a friend of his going by and he called him. He asked the friend to help him to remove an apparatus from the boot and without hesitation, the friend helped them. Laxmi then came with three mugs of tea and some cakes and Michael's friend accepted gratefully, as well as the others. Soon, Michael was busy with his work.

Sunil and his wife Renu came and Renu went inside to talk to Laxmi while Sunil remained outside talking to Dev and Michael. Michael told him that day after tomorrow, he can come, there will be electric lights in the house. Sunil said that he will come as he is thinking to have a generator installed at his place as well.

The following day, Dev was still at home when Michael arrived to continue with his job. Dev wished him good luck that he will finish the work quickly and he went to The Shop.

Dev again asked his messenger to get the newspapers and he went through them, especially about the robbery at the Planters Bank. Speculation was rife as to the manner in which the robbery was committed and the persons involved.

The corpse of the deceased was handed over to the relatives for burial. The accused who was in custody was denying that there were three persons involved in the alleged robbery, they were only two of them to try to remove some money but they could not do it as the watchmen were there and one of them shot at his friend. The Policemen did not believe the accused's version of what had happened.

After one week in custody, the accused came up with a version that the Police accepted as plausible. He said, "The person who died was called Jean. He was my good friend and we were residing near to each other. We were having a drink and some food in the bar at the corner of Farquhar and Sir William Newton Streets. Another man came and he sat at the table next to ours. He also ordered a drink and then he started talking to us. He got us interested in what he has done in life, which if believed, appears to be very interesting. He asked about us, and we told him what we had done. We exaggerated a bit but then he told us who we were and what we really had done, which was not much. Then he proposed a coup that he had prepared, to enter into a bank and rob a huge sum. We were tempted by the money. We asked him what his name was, but he refused to give any particulars of himself and told us that we shall know about him later on. We were to accompany him and we shall get our share.

"On the cyclonic night, we met at a previously arranged place near the Treasury Building at about one o'clock at night. We met the man there. The cyclone was at its peak. Nobody but ourselves only could be seen all around. We moved towards the Planters Bank very slowly as the gusts of wind were strong and we could easily get carried away, we had to stop every now and then and get some shelter from the wind. Eventually, we arrived at the Bank. Reaching there, we saw that the main door was damaged. Maybe the cyclone was responsible for the damage. Or maybe the man had caused the damage to the door before he came to meet us, I do not know.

"When we entered the bank, we did not see any watchman, but still we were moving slowly. The man had a torch with him. We went downstairs. The two watchmen were surprised to see us, but the man with us pointed a revolver at them and told them to lie down on the floor and he made them smell something. The two watchmen were quiet and they fell asleep, as if dead. I and my friend were scared that the watchmen had died, we asked the man who was with us, but he assured us that they were alright. We had never participated in a murder case, and we were not going to do it this time. The strong room was also damaged and so was the safe. We removed a lot of money.

The man who was with us told us that he will keep the money upstairs and then he will come downstairs again and then we can go out and each one will get a share. We were waiting for the man to come back, but in the meantime, one of the watchmen woke up and without saying anything, fired two shots at my friend who fell down, wounded as far as I can recollect. I was then on the stairs with my hands on my head. My hands were then tied with a piece of string by one of the watchmen and I was made to lie down in a corner. In the morning I saw Policemen in the Bank and I was taken to the Station.

"I do not know the man who made the plan to rob the bank, I also do not know the name of the man nor where he resides. If I see him again, I can recognize him. The Police did not secure any money from me, or any house-breaking tools."

The statement was supposedly read over to the alleged maker, he signed it, voluntarily as was mentioned, and then he was given a cigarette after eight days. He was grateful for that and also for the fact that the pressure on him was released. He was taken to the Court twice since his arrest. Two days later, he was taken to the Court for a third time and from there he was remanded to the Prison.

Two matters arise for consideration. To start with, the Police are always in a hurry to arrest those who have committed crimes and get them to give their statements in which they confess having committed the offences. Then the enquiry is closed. If the persons arrested do not want to confess, then it is not surprising that stronger tactics are made use of, and when such tactics are used, you find even hardened criminals succumbing. It all depends on who uses those third degree tactics. The enquiry ends and subsequently, the case is submitted to the Director of Public Prosecutions.

In the course of the proceedings, the person arrested is remanded to Prison, though he has not been judged by the relevant Court. He is called a prisoner on remand, why a prisoner it is difficult to say. He is called a prisoner on remand, though the two words cannot go together. A person can be on remand, but then he cannot be a prisoner. But the wider question is why a person not yet convicted is sent to prison when we know that a person on remand is under the responsibility of the Commissioner of Police, whereas a person who has been judged by a Magistrate or a Judge and found guilty and sentenced to a term of imprisonment is under the responsibility of the Commissioner of Prisons?

So the person alleged to be involved in the bank robbery was sent to prison. Here he had time to reflect upon his destiny, what wrong did he do? Some persons in prison befriended him and he talked freely and openly to them. He told them that he is accused of robbing a bank and his friend was killed. But was this the truth? Definitely not, but who will listen to him? There is nobody to believe in what he was saying.

In prison, some more inmates started talking to him, most of them wanted to know how much money he stole from the bank and more specifically, where he has hidden the booty. The two friends with whom he could talk quite openly could be trusted and he confided in them. When he gave the name of the Police Inspector who conducted the inquiry into the case, one of the friends laughed. He said, "You confessed for a crime that you did not do, but you voluntarily put your signature on the document, after it had been allegedly read over to you. The confession was countersigned by another

Police officer and how is it that you now say that the confession is not yours?"

Every now and then he was taken to court and simply remanded again to prison. In the meantime, his relatives contacted a barrister, but they could not pay the fees of the learned counsel. They tried another one, but again with this one also, it was the same. He was still in prison.

13.....THEY ARE GETTING READY TO START A NEW LIFE

Long Kader had been to see Dev and Dev took him to the Municipal Council of Port Louis to meet one of his friends. He talked to him and explained that Kader wanted to have a plan for a house made as quickly as possible. He said, "You know, his house has been destroyed in the cyclone, he has started to get rid of the rubble and the rubbish, in fact of everything lying on the ground. "

The officer asked "Let us have a look at your title deed and your site plan."

"Unfortunately, all his documents have been destroyed. What can be done now? The title deed is in the name of his mother."

"He must get a copy of the title deed and a copy of the site plan. In the meantime, I can go to the Registration Office and get the necessary details from the registers. However, today I cannot do anything, if he is really in a hurry, he can come and see me during lunchtime tomorrow and I will see what can be done. But I will do it essentially for you, Dev. Do not say that I am not helping you."

"I have never said so."

"You must tell me what kind of a house you want to construct, how many rooms and such other details. Get ready by tomorrow," so said the officer to Kader.

They then went to The Shop. Dev told Kader, "I would advise you to construct your building, where you will actually live in the rear and in the front, have a commercial section.

You remember you told me that you had about one hundred and ten toises of land. That is quite a large portion of land in the area where you live. Some people in the area do not have half of that extent, and yet they are satisfied."

"Two persons I have employed will clear off the land of all the rubbles and tomorrow a friend will help me to put up a small lean-to and I can sleep there. By the way, I have talked to my mother and she agrees that I must try to construct a house. In fact, she was delighted that now I am becoming a real man."

Dev then explained what type of building he had in mind for him. Let the plan be for a storied house. But construct only the ground floor now. One day, God willing, you will be able to afford the storied part also. Now you can go to the Planters Bank, talk to somebody you know and ask him if they can give you a housing loan because your house has been completely destroyed. You tell him that you can give your land as a guarantee for the repayment of the loan. From there you go to the Mauritius Housing Corporation where you will tell them that you need a loan as soon as possible. From there you go to the State Bank of Mauritius for the same purpose. You understand what I am saying?"

"Yes, Mr Dev, I will do that."

"But right now you go and see Suren Bridgelal, the notary. He is my cousin, you tell him that… Anyway, let me ring him up." He rang up Suren and said, "Suren, Dev here. Do me a favour. I am sending somebody to see you, try to help him…His house has been destroyed in the cyclone and he has lost all his documents and he needs a copy of the title deed and also a copy of the site plan. Can you help him? That will be part of your social work…If you can make a request immediately…OK, I am sending him to your Chambers immediately. Thanks Suren…."

Dev told him to go immediately, his cousin the notary would be waiting for him. He would be closing his office in half an hour. Things were moving well in so far as Long Kader was concerned. What would Michael be doing?

Dev arrived at his place around half past four. Michael was busy with the installation of the generator. He told Dev, "By tomorrow, I will be completing with the job."

"I thought that today I will have some electricity in at least in some rooms. Well, if nothing can be done for today, we will have to manage without electricity for another day."

"I can work for another hour, I see what can be done."

Dev went inside his house and soon he came out with two mugs of tea. Michael had his tea and he continued working at the same time. Around seven o'clock, Michael told him that it was time to test run the generator. He put the machine on and told Dev to switch the light on in the sitting room. Immediately, there was electricity and Laxmi was so happy. And she put the ceiling fan on. Dev went out to tell Michael that the sitting room was well lighted now and he thanked him profusely.

Michael told him, "I will advise you to put on the lights in your TV room and in your bedroom. You can put your TV on of course. Do not make an abuse of the electricity. I will come and complete what remains to be done tomorrow morning."

When Michael was gone, Neela came to speak to Dev, "Mr Dev, deduct the cost of the window panes from my pay at the end of the month, if you do not mind. Mr Dev, I will have to help my son because he told me that he did not have enough money to purchase what he needs for his children. As a mother I cannot refuse him, for the sake of the children."

"There is no problem, Neela. You are still here today? I thought that at this time, you will be at your place, anyway, I will drop you."

Laxmi said, "Neela, you can stay here to-night. You have no electricity at your place, what will you do in the dark? Here you can watch television. Do stay." Laxmi can be very persuasive at times and this was one of such occasions. They had their dinner while watching news on the television. Thereafter, Dev asked Laxmi to come for a drive and she requested Neela to come along. They drove to the place of Sunil, and members of his family were sitting in their front yard. Three chairs were brought and Dev informed them that they had electricity at their place, and they could come anytime they felt like it. Sunil asked him if it was worth having the generator.

Dev replied, "Definitely. According to me, we do not know when the Central Electricity Board people will complete the repairs and the verification of all the electricity lines."

Sunil said, "When will the electrician come to your place? I think that I will go for the same type of generator as the one you have at your place."

"You can come tomorrow around six o'clock. I will ask him to drop in."

And they went back home. The next day, it was sunny and hot. Laxmi asked Neela to wash all the different items of clothing, some curtains and other items and the clothes lines were soon all taken up. She opened all the doors and windows and there was a slight breeze. It was nice to be in the house, and it was drying very fast.

Dev had a part-time gardener who used to come once every week. That day was the day. He came and immediately started cleaning the garden of the leaves, small branches and whatever was brought in the yard by the cyclone. The gardener was a very fast worker, faster than anybody else, and Dev used to say that it was a pleasure to just watch him at his job. He worked for three hours and the yard was better looking than it was before the cyclone. Laxmi gave him a mug of tea and a piece of bread and butter. She had this habit of giving at least a mug of tea to any person who came to her place. Because of the force of habit, she did not even ask whether the person will like a mug of tea, she assumed that he would. Every day she brews so many mugs that she has become an expert in the art of tea making.

Dev did not go to the shop that day, so he went to buy the papers and sat down to read them. By then Michael had completed the installation and asked him to verify what he had done. Dev was satisfied. He said, "Michael, there is no need for me to verify what you have done. I trust you. Is it possible for you to drop in around six o'clock? My brother-in-law will come to meet you because he has decided to have a generator installed at his place as well.”

The following day, Michael came to Dev’s place at half past eight and together they entered in the car. It was clear that Michael wanted to talk to him. As soon as they were on the road, he said, “You know, Mr Dev, there is a very old house in which two old persons are living. Surprisingly, that old house has not been blown down in the cyclone, though some windows have been damaged, and a few iron sheets have become loose. Of course there have been some damaged planks by the rain that have to be replaced immediately. However, I think that the house has to be pulled down.”

“Are they prepared to sell the land?”

“They told me to look for somebody who is prepared to buy their property. I told them that the house is not worth buying but I told them that I will try to talk to people who would be interested. And I asked them how much they were expecting the property to fetch. And they told me that they will sell for one million rupees. And they told me that they will give me a good commission in case I will get a client.”

“Where is that house in relation to your place?”

“At about ten minutes’ walk from my place. It is away from the cite, three streets away. There are two big mango trees in the yard, most of the branches have been detached from the trees and there is disorder all over the place. I am wondering how such a house has been able to withstand the cyclone.”

“If you are interested to buy the property, I have my idea on it. Go and tell them that you are interested to buy their house yourself. The couple would be surprised that a Creole like you would be interested to buy a property, but you tell them that you are serious, that you work hard and that you have saved some money. Then you ask them what is the last price for which they would be prepared to part with their property. Maybe they will say that for you they can make a concession. They will say about nine hundred thousand rupees. You tell them that you can give them eight hundred thousand rupees. They will ask you how will be paying? You tell them that you will be taking a loan. And you tell them that you will come the next day.

"The next day you go there and ask them if they had thought over the matter and if they say they have, and maybe they will tell you that they are in a hurry, you tell them that in two weeks you can be ready. And tell them that you have something important to convey to them. Tell them that if the contract of sale will not mention the sale price as being eight hundred thousand rupees, but say six hundred rupees, you will be able to save some money. Probably they will agree.

"Your regular bank is in Quatre Bornes I take it? Deposit a sum of say eighty thousand rupees in your account, today itself if possible. You have a credit balance in your account?"

"Yes, I have about thirty thousand in my account."

By then they had reached The Shop. Dev removed a sum of one hundred thousand from the hidden safe. He handed it to Michael and told him to deposit eighty thousand and keep twenty thousand for his expenses. "I would kindly request you not get drunk, I am saying this in your own interest. Now sign a document that you have received that sum."

Michael then went to meet the Blackburn couple who owned the property. After some preliminary discussions, an agreement was reached. They also had no objection to receiving two hundred thousand rupees outside the contract, "under the table" as they termed it. "Most persons who buy or sell property resort to this trick, and in this way, they pay less by way of registration duty. The notaries know about this as well as those in the Courts." Defrauding the authorities of the different taxes is a criminal offence, but people do not consider it to be so, on the contrary, those involved therein are looked upon as good businessmen.

Long Kader went to see the clerk at the municipality for the plan of the house. He gave the details that the clerk asked for and he was surprised that the land belonged to the mother. He got the confirmation that the house would be constructed in the name of the mother. He asked Kader to come back in an hour's time and the clerk went to the registration office.

Kader just went for a short walk in the area where he usually does his business as a street hawker. A few of his friends had started work, and they asked him when he will start? He told them that he has no house, the stock, the little that he had, has been lost in the cyclone. His house has been completely destroyed and now he will try to get a loan and construct a small house, but it must be in concrete. He will start working the following week.

When he went back to the municipality, the clerk was making rough sketches. He asked Kader what kind on building he wanted to construct. Kader told him that he would like the front part of the building as a shop, if it would be possible that part to have two rooms, then he would like to have the residential part at the rear. This would have three bedrooms, a sitting room, a kitchen, a TV room, a corridor, a verandah, a bathroom, a WC and a place for ironing clothes.

"You have done the necessary to get a copy of the title deed and of the site plan? The land is of an extent of one hundred and ten toises, and the title is clear."

"My mother owns the land and I am her only child. I hope to construct this building and give her some comfort in her old age. I owe her that much at least, for she has done so much for me."

"You tell my friend Dev that in about five days, a sketch of the plan will be ready. You come and see me say day after tomorrow around the same time."

Long Kader went to report to Dev the progress of the drawing of the plan, and Dev rang up the municipal clerk. He thanked him for the speed at which he is working. He told him that he could come to the shop for a chat and it was agreed that he could come the day after tomorrow; they then could have a chat and look at the sketch of the plan at the same time. There was no need for his friend to see him at the municipality on that day. He would be at The Shop.

Dev told Kader to deposit two hundred thousand rupees in his account at the bank today itself. He took out that sum from the hidden safe and made him sign a document for the sum. The band securing the notes were torn off and then secured with an elastic band and he was asked to come back immediately thereafter.

Dev was satisfied with his three employees at the shop. They were doing their best, to the satisfaction of Dev. Though he did not appear to be that interested in the shop, in fact he was keeping a keen eye as to how the shop was being run and could not find any major shortcoming. The understanding between the employer and the employees was as it should be, and their relationship was more or less friendly. The employees liked it when Dev showed that he was concerned about them, but not only about the employees, but also about their families. So the relationship went on strengthening.

Around six o'clock, Sunil came to Dev's to meet Michael the electrician and it was agreed that he also would have a generator installed at his place and he asked whether Michael would come tomorrow to purchase it. Michael looked at Dev and asked, "Are you going to the shop tomorrow? I can meet Mister Sunil in Port Louis in that case."

Of course he will go to Port Louis and it was decided that Sunil would meet the electrician at about ten o'clock in The Shop. Michael wanted to talk to Dev but he had not had the opportunity to do so. He therefore left and the relatives talked for some time about the effects of the cyclone and then Sunil and his wife also left.

The following morning, Michael was in the car with Dev. He told him, "Mr Dev, I have been to see Mr and Mrs Blackburn for the house. They accept to sell it for eight hundred thousand rupees and they also have no objection to have the contract drawn up for six hundred thousand. But there is one problem. How to get the eight hundred thousand rupees at one go?"

"We shall look for a solution to your problem," so replied Dev. Michael then told Dev that he would have to buy certain spare parts for his job and that he would be back before ten o'clock.

When Sunil came Dev showed him the generator that he had installed and Sunil asked him if he was satisfied with its performance? Dev told him that he had used it only once, during the night of the cyclone and he can't complain.

When Long Kader came back, Dev introduced him to Sunil and told Sunil that his house had been completed destroyed and now he had to build a new house but this time he would have to get a concrete house.

"Have you got the relevant forms for the loan?" he asked Kader.

"Here are the forms, but I do not know if I can get the loan. The clerk at the bank asked me whether I had a portion of land which will be the guarantee for the loan and I had to tell him that the land is in my mother's name. He told me to fill in these forms."

"Now go to the State Commercial Bank and to the Mauritius Housing Corporation and tell them the same thing. Ask them what rate of interest they charge for a housing loan. You come to see me tomorrow at noon and my friend from the municipality will be here for your plan. There is no need for you to go to his office."

When Michael came, Sunil went with him to buy his generator. Now Dev was free to find out how the shop was doing. Business had come to a sudden standstill following the cyclone but it had started picking up. He talked to two of his employees about his idea of stocking some more of the fast moving items. He then rang up a gentleman by the name of Shree Reetoo. He was the manufacturer of articles well appreciated by the tourists. He ordered what he needed and they had to argue about the date of delivery and eventually a date suitable to both parties was agreed upon. Dev decided to go home early because he was feeling tired. But before leaving, he asked for some Dal Puris for lunch. He was eating them when Long Kader came and reported that this morning he had no problem to deposit the one hundred thousand rupees in the bank. He then went to the other banks.

When Dev reached home, Laxmi was surprised that he came so early. He said he was tired and went to bed. There was no electricity in Quatre Bornes yet and nearly everyone was living in darkness except for the usual candle light. Dev is not a person who can stay at home, Laxmi knew of this. When he woke up, she wanted to know whether he wants to go somewhere. If not, he can call one or two of his friends with their families and they can discuss about the affairs of the Temple. Dev agreed but suggested that Sunil also should be included in the discussion. The wives of the friends of Dev were also good friends of Laxmi and the husbands of the friends of Laxmi were also the friends of Dev.

Talks of the effect of the cyclone went on for some time, then they started discussing about the Temple of which they were members. They kept on talking on the subject till about eleven at night and then they parted.

The following morning Dev arrived at the shop early. He then went to see his brother who lives near the Champ de Mars. He is a doctor, a good one, and he is in private practice. After the usual news exchanges, Indra, for that was his name, asked Dev how he was feeling. He is the younger brother and they have a very good relationship. Indra's wife came to talk about the cyclone and about the family and then left.

Dev told him, "Why do you ask about how I am feeling? I am feeling alright, I wonder why you have put such a question? Anyway, as you have put the question, you can check my blood pressure." The blood pressure was checked, it was a bit on the high side, sixteen over ten. He verified his blood sugar which was normal. Mauritians are known the world over that they are first among the diabetes sufferers and Indra was careful that Dev might be a victim of this disease.

Dev then told him that he was feeling tired yesterday, should he go for a blood test?

"It would be a good idea, I'll give you a letter which you can hand over to our friend Cheong and he will send me the result."

"Do you think that I should see a cardiologist: Just for a check-up?"

"Oh yes, I would advise you to do it. Go and pay a visit to Dr Rajen. He is one of the best cardiologists we know."

Dev had always been very concerned about his health. A slight fever or some pain would cause him to see a doctor.

And he has become quite an expert concerning medicines. He gives advice to people who want to know what they are suffering from and then he tells them what doctor they should see.

He came back to the shop where Kader was waiting for him. He had with him the documents from the State Commercial Bank as well as from The Mauritius Housing Corporation. The preferred to take a loan either from the Mauritius Housing Corporation or the State Commercial Bank. The clerk from the municipality came to see Dev. After the usual greetings, the clerk said, "I have brought the rough drawings of the plan of the house." And he presented the sheets of paper to Dev. Dev and Kader had a close look.

"Is it possible to have a plan that would accommodate a ground floor and two additional floors? The two upstairs floors would not be constructed immediately of course. Let us concentrate on the ground floor to start with. This is urgent."

"Of course it can be done. The residential part and the commercial part would be two sections of the same building, you agree with this. Now you must give me whatever further instructions you have in mind, because I will start with the plan in the final stages."

Dev asked Kader whether he was satisfied with the plan and Kader answered that it could not have been better. Except that in the commercial part the two rooms could have a removable separation or if better, there might be a corridor." This was noted by the clerk. He said that he must have the documents by next week and then the plan can be submitted for approval to the authorities.

Dev asked the clerk where he considers it better for Kader to get a loan for the construction. And the reply was "No doubt it should be the MHC or the SCB."

Dev told Kader to pay the clerk for his work. He went out for two minutes and let the two discuss how much Kader should pay for drawing up the plan.

Thereafter, Dev went to see the doctor who would analyse his blood, and then he went to see his cardiologist. They were relatives and both of them were great conversationalists and they spent more time talking of other matters than of the state of Dev's heart. At last, the good doctor said that his heart was perfect condition, taking into consideration Dev's age and the antecedent concerning his health. Dev went home and told Laxmi about what he had done during the day. Laxmi was somewhat angry with him, because he had not told her that he was not feeling well and he had had to consult three doctors.

Electricity was re-established on the main road of Quatre Bornes as well as in certain sections of Port Louis, Rose Hill, Vacoas and Curepipe. In the villages also work was going on at full speed and maybe in another fortnight nearly the whole country would be supplied with electricity and this thanks to the help of the foreign workers who had been sent by the friendly countries.

Work on the roads, especially the removal of the trees and branches that had fallen right on the roads, was going on smoothly. There were complaints by quite a number of people that the authorities were neglecting them, but they would not understand that everything could not be done at the same time.

14…..A PERSON BUYS A PORTION OF LAND

The following day, Michael came to see Dev in the shop. He was taking this idea of buying a property seriously. "We must move fast, otherwise Mr Blackburn might sell the property to another buyer."

Dev told him "We would like to give him the two hundred thousand rupees 'under the table' as they say; this will keep the Blackburn happy. But we must make them sign a document to the effect that both Mr and Mrs Blackburn will sell their property for eight hundred thousand rupees and as an avaloir, as an advance on the sale price, you have paid him two hundred thousand rupees on a particular date. The balance will be paid when the contract of sale will be finalized and that this should be in a month's time."

Then they went to see the cousin of Dev, the notary. Dev told him that Michael wanted to buy a property and he must be ready to be the notary in this matter. He wanted to have a copy of the title deed of the vendor and certain particulars. Dev told Michael that he has to ask Blackburn for his title deed in order to effect searches at the Registration Office so that the contact of sale will be prepared. The notary was very particular about the legal side of all transactions. Dev told him that he will talk to his clerk Dilip about a certain matter.

Dev and Michael went to talk to Dilip. Dev told him "Michael will be buying a property for eight hundred thousand rupees, but he would like to have the contract drawn up for six hundred thousand, and the two hundred thousand will be paid outside the contract. I know that you can draw up such a document, so do me a favour and prepare it as soon as possible."

"It will be a document between the two parties. It cannot be registered and the real contract will have to be finalized and completed within a given date. It will be only a sort of security for finalizing the transaction."

When they were back in the shop, Dev asked Michael whether he was satisfied with what has happened so far. The eyes of the latter became moist and he could not say anything. He then said that he would be going to get the document off Mr Blackburn and then he would go the place of Mr Sunil for the installation of the generator. He said that he was hoping that the mason will have completed with his part of the job.

Dev started to devote some more time to the shop, went over his stock with the help of one of the employees. Those items that were lying in the shop for some time, for which there was a slow demand, would be put on sale at a discount price of twenty per cent.

A decision taken by the government was announced to the public. "Following the passage of cyclone Mady in which many residential buildings have been damaged and others have been completely destroyed, government has taken the decision to help those whose houses have been completely destroyed by facilitating the approval of their plans in case they want to reconstruct their buildings through a fast track procedure and they will obtain loan facilities that will be disbursed as quickly as possible. Those persons whose houses have been damaged will be given some material to carry out the necessary repairs. The officers of the Ministry of Housing and Lands have been specially detailed to help those who need any relevant help." Other information followed.

On the next day, Kader came to see Dev in the shop quite early. Dev told him, "You should forget about getting a loan from the SCB, you must concentrate essentially on the MHC. But you should first go to the Ministry of Housing and Lands to declare that your mother's house has been completely destroyed. Maybe an officer will come to visit the site where the house was situated. Tell them that the house belonged to your mother, or better still take your mother with you when you will go to the Ministry. When will you get title deed to the land?"

"Maybe day after tomorrow. This is what the notary had told me."

"Today it's Thursday, you can fill in your form for the loan."

Dev took the form from Kader and started filling it in but he said that unless there is a copy of the title deed he cannot complete the request.

"Anyway, let us complete the form to the extent possible. Leave the forms here and you go to the Ministry with your mother. I will see you on Friday. Go to the notary's to find out whether the copy of title deed and the plan of the site have been obtained from the Registrar General's office. You must make four or five photo copies because you will need them."

Kader said, "I go on my business for two or three hours every day. I do not want to send a message that I am not working. My colleagues know that I have lost my house and that I have already cleared the land and that I am trying to get a loan to construct another house. Now I will be going to attend to my business and at about two o'clock, I will go to the ministry." With that, he left the shop.

Since the cyclone hit the country the weather had turned mild. It was not so hot as before and a smooth and cool breeze was blowing, which made a walk in the streets of Port Louis a pleasure.

Dev was talking to somebody in the shop when Indar came to see him. They both went in the sitting room and Indar asked him, "How are you feeling today? By looks, I will say that you are better than yesterday."

"I feel much better today."

"But I do think that you must not get over busy. What did Dr. Rajen say about your heart condition?"

"He said that everything is fine, there is no need to worry."

"Laxmi rang me up to tell me to talk to you and I was about to visit you, so I have come to satisfy myself and Laxmi as well." He rang up Laxmi and told her not to worry about the health condition of Dev. Of course he must not smoke, but will he listen to you or to me, for that matter?"

Dev said, "Let me speak to her." He took the phone from Indar and in the phone he said, "Why do you bother everybody for nothing? You know I am alright...I have not been very occupied, I am just trying to help just two persons. That's all I am doing. I shall be coming home in a little while. Tomorrow you can come with me in the shop, you can see for yourself how busy I am...Of course I'll drop you at the place of Indar." Dev rang off and said to Indar "Well, tomorrow Laxmi will be coming with me and she wants to spend the day at your place."

"It will be a pleasure, bring her as soon as you will come down to Port Louis."

Dev asked him, "You know Long Kader, whose father was working with father?"

"Of course I remember him. It's a long time that I have not seen him. I know that he is a street hawker."

"He lost his house in the cyclone and I am trying to help him in his demarches for the reconstruction. That is one person I am trying to help. The other person is my electrician who has decided to buy a portion of land."

"He is a Creole I take it. Can he pay for the land? Do not fall into any trap; otherwise you will be left holding the baby."

"You also still have this prejudice? It is time for you to change your outlook. You will see this man working and then pronounce your judgment."

On Friday, Dev came down to the shop around nine o'clock. Laxmi was with him and the employees greeted her and asked her how she was in the cyclone and whether everything is under control at home. Laxmi replied politely and asked each of the employees about their respective families and then went in the office where Dev was looking at some papers. She sat down and talked to him about the progress of the shop during the past year and both of them were satisfied that the shop was giving them a very good return. After half an hour, Dev dropped her at the place of Indar and came back to the shop. Michael was waiting for him.

He informed Dev that Mr Blackburn is insistent to know when the contract will be signed and when can I give him some advance money. I told him that I must give the document to my notary and then he will prepare the contract after verifying that there will be no problem. So he gave me this document."

"Very good. Take it to the notary and just give it to him. And then see if Dilip has prepared the document that he has to prepare. It would be better to hand this document first to Dilip, he also will need it. When he has done with it, then leave it with the notary."

Dilip phoned up Dev and it was decided that he would be ready with the document by the next day. He does not work on Saturdays. Dev said, "So you are free to bring the document to my place and I will take you to the place of Blackburn to have it signed. Say around one o'clock."

Dev knew Dilip well as they also are related.

Michael came back to The Shop and he informed Dev that he must go back to Sunil's place for the installation of the generator. Dev told him that Dilip would be at his place at one o'clock and they would go to the place of Mr Blackburn together. Take two hundred thousand rupees to give to Mr Blackburn but you must be careful that you do not lose the money or more importantly, your relatives must not know that you have so much money with you. They will want to know where you got it from and they will want to spend it immediately."

Dev removed two hundred thousand rupees from the hidden safe, and handed the sum to Michael and made him sign on a document. He said that he will be going directly to do some work and left.

Then it was the turn of Kader to come to the shop and he was accompanied with his mother. She was old, but very erect and thin. She was very nice to Dev. She kissed him on both cheeks, wept a little bit and Dev asked her how she was. She said that life was going on very slowly, but she has had some problems with Kader.

Dev told her, "Do not worry about him, I am looking after him now, I will see to it that he does not move around with people who will make him do what he must not. He must understand that he should never go to prison again."

"You will be a good influence on him. And now he is telling me that he wants to construct a house on the land that we have. Is this a good idea? I have come to ask you about this, but my main purpose is that I had not seen you for a long time. I really wanted to see you. And how I would like to meet your brother!"

Dev told her, "Indar was here yesterday and he was asking about Kader. About the house, I will say that it is a very good idea. Kader can get a loan which he can reimburse in small instalments. The house and the loan will be in your name, but Kader will guarantee everything. You should not worry about anything, you have had enough worries to last you for two entire lives. It is time for you to look after your grandchildren, but for that, Kader must get married."

Kader's mother replied, "Kader must become serious first, he should not associate with those who drive him on the wrong path, only then can he think of getting married. He is not becoming younger, and he does not understand how I would like to see two or three children in my house." And here she wept, not for the show but rather she let her heart cry. She was serious.

Kader said, "We have been to the Ministry and we explained our situation. An officer said that he will visit our area on Monday next and I should be on the site at nine o'clock."

"Let us hope that by then we can have a copy of your title deed. If you can get it, then take it with you on the site."

Slowly and slowly, electricity was being provided to certain areas in the towns as well as the countryside. More than half of Port Louis was already lighted up. Vacoas likewise was already provided and it was said that in another three of four days, interruption of electric supply in the area would be a thing of the past.

Dev read a religious book, the Katha Upanishad, for about an hour. By then Laxmi rang him up to request him that they are waiting for him to come and have lunch. He went to Indar's place where he had lunch with the other members of the family. Dev informed them that Kader's mother came to see him and she was asking him about Indar.

"She is a very nice woman and for us she was like a mother for the attention that she had for us. You must see her one of these days, she will be so happy, besides you were her favourite when we were young."

15.....THE SHOP IS DOING WELL

The next day, it was a Saturday and usually, Dev does not go to the shop, he likes to stay in bed till around eight o'clock. But this Saturday, it was different. He was up early and got busy with some paperwork. At one o'clock, Dilip came and he was talking to Laxmi and soon Michael came as well. Laxmi went inside.

Dev and the two others discussed about the payment of the two hundred thousand rupees and the document that will be signed. Then they went in the car of Dev to the place of Mr Blackburn. This latter was surprised to see Dev, because they knew each other well. After some exchange of news, they started talking of business. Dilip who was introduced by Dev as a notary's clerk, explained what the agreement was. Nobody raised any objection.

Then Dev said, "Edwin, is it possible for Michael to pay six hundred thousand say in three months' time? You see, otherwise he will have to negotiate for a loan and you know the conditions that they impose before they give you a loan are simply loaded in their favour."

Edwin Blackburn answered, "In other circumstances, I would never refuse such a request coming from you. You know my eldest son Clency. He is in Australia. He has now called us to stay with him. My wife insists that we should try to live the end of our lives in that country where so many of our people are well settled. And in two months' time, we must be in Australia, otherwise our visa will expire. In these circumstances, is it possible to give the buyer a delay to pay us the total of the sale price?"

"I do understand. He will pay on the date due," countered Dev.

"I would like to tell you that if I will not feel at ease in Australia or if I will miss the atmosphere of Mauritius, I will be back in no time" countered Edwin Blackburn.

The document was signed by the two parties and the money was handed over to John Blackburn. They were about to leave when Dev asked Blackburn what he would do with the furniture in the house, and he was told that they will have to be sold, if possible.

"Are you interested in any of the items? If yes, do tell me and I will give them to you at throw away prices, but with one proviso, that you can collect them only on the day I will be leaving the country. If you agree, come and have a look in the different rooms. All of them did have a look and Dev said "in a few days, I will come and see you Edwin. I will then tell you what items of furniture will be of interest to me."

In the car while coming back Dev said "My wife does not want me to buy antiques, be they furniture or whatever else. She considers them as second hand things and says that her parents never used to buy second hand things. It is not now that she will accept such things. But I saw the furniture in the house of Blackburn and I could not resist from trying to make an offer. And then there were some books in the bookshelf that I would like to have."

Dilip requested Dev to drop him at the bus stop as he had to be at home in an hour's time. Dev stopped the car near the bus stop and he told Michael to pay Dilip for his efforts and he got out of the car and went to buy a paper. When he came back, Dilip thanked him and Dev left to go to his place.

Michael said, "Mr Dev, you must not give me such a big burden. Last night I could not sleep at all. I kept thinking of the money, now I feel light and I am sure that I will be able to sleep soundly."

"Now you have to pay to Blackburn six hundred thousand rupees. Right?"

"Yes, Mr Dev. At the moment I have in the bank two hundred thousand rupees."

"You must deposit in the bank another one hundred thousand on Monday and talk to the manager that you need a loan of three hundred thousand rupees as you are going to purchase a piece of land. You tell him that you have a sum of three thousand rupees in your account and you are prepared to give him the portion of land as guarantee. He will give you the money, maybe he will think that you as a Creole will not be able to pay back the loan and therefore he will buy the property from you at a very cheap price. He will be in for a shock when you will reimburse him the loan before the date due. Don't tell about the land transaction to anybody."

In the afternoon, Dev and Laxmi went to their good friend's place and Sunil and his wife also came. Now that electricity was established in the area, life was returning back to normal. They were all people of the middle or upper middle classes and they had always been used to leading a different kind of life when compared to people of a different class. They understood other people as other people understood them. They lived their lives as they thought fit and they preferred not to meddle in the manner in which others lived. Their relationship was very formal but they were not on friendly terms with others. There was no enmity-type of relationship between them, nor any type of hatred.

They had a long chat on everything possible, there was laughter and of course they indulged in some gossip. Do not think that only women gossip. Men gossip as much, if not more than, women.

On the following Monday, Michael went to see Dev in the shop. And this latter gave him another hundred thousand rupees and Dev told him "When you go to the bank, see that you do not deal with the same clerk as last time. And do not forget to talk to the manager about the loan. Tell him that you are in a hurry for the loan as the vendor will be migrating to Australia."

In the afternoon, Kader came to report to him. He stated, "This morning, the officer from the ministry came on the site. My mother was there as well and my mother said that the land is hers, they have always lived here and this violent cyclone took away their house. If he can help us to rebuild the house, we shall be most grateful to him and to the government. I then told her to keep quiet as she talks too much.

"The officer asked me how can he be sure that there was a house there before the cyclone? I said that he can ask anybody in the area and they will confirm that the house was here before the coming of the cyclone. The officer was satisfied and even commended me for having cleared the land so fast.

"And my mother was simply touched when she saw you after I do not know how many years. She kept talking about you, your brother and your father and more so about your mother. Now she has picked up some fresh energy and she wants to get me married."

Dev asked him if he had received the title deed and the site plan. He said "Yes, Mr Dev. I have the original and four photocopies." He had them in an envelope and he gave them to Dev. Dev took a copy, read it and then had a look at the site plan." He started to fill in the forms of the MHC and it took some time to do that. It was decided that Kader's mother would ask for a loan of either seven or eight hundred thousand rupees. Kader wanted to sign the forms but Dev said that the application should be made in the name of his mother. He would have to get her signature as well as a document from the ministry that her house has been completely destroyed in the cyclone.

"So you must get a document from the Ministry of Housing and Lands certifying that her house has been completely destroyed by the cyclone and that she is entitled to get a loan for the construction of a building in replacement of the destroyed building.

"Now we must find out whether the plan is ready. Go to the municipality and talk to my friend there. Give him a copy of the title deed and a copy of the site plan. Ask him what you must do next. Ask him for a copy of the plan and ask him when it can be submitted for approval." With those instructions, Kader went about what he had to do, but he told Dev that he would do some business first.

Kader went to the place on the pavement where he usually sells his wares and was busy for about two hours. Then he went to the ministry where he looked for the officer who had come to visit his portion of land. Eventually he came across him but he told Kader that he was going to perform outdoor duties. Kader looked at him in a very miserable manner and the officer relented and took him to his office. He filled in a form and signed it before handing it Kader. He said "Have two or three copies made and annex a copy with your loan application and another copy to your plan that you will submit for approval. I hope that you will not have problems to get your loan and the approval of the plan." Kader was very grateful to the officer and thanked him profusely.

Then he went to the municipality where he had to wait for the officer concerned. The officer came back half an hour later. And told him to come back on the following day but before leaving, Kader gave him a copy of the document from the Ministry of Housing and Lands and the officer told him, "I will attach it to your plan. In the meantime, you have to get the permit from the CEB and the CWA. However, I do not think that you will have any problem from these two authorities as you already were a consumer before the cyclone."

Subsequently, he went to the MHC to hand over the form for the loan. After a short wait, he was received by a clerk. Kader explained to him "I live in Plaine Verte. I was living with my mother but the house in which we were living was completely destroyed during the cyclone. I am now requesting for a loan. I have already filled in the forms and now I have come to submit them. I also have a certificate from the Ministry of Housing and Lands."

He handed him all the documents and the clerk had a look at them and told Kader "You must give me a copy of the plan of the building which you propose to construct."

Kader asked him, "Do you think that I have to wait for the plan and then resubmit all the documents together or can I leave those that I have with me now and later on I will bring the plan?"

"You can leave with me the documents that you have now. I am going to open a file for you. You know that we have been instructed to treat applications such as yours in a fast track. Complete all your documentation and we shall act fast in your case."

Kader thereafter called on Dev to report on the progress that had been made on the various demarches undertaken. Both of them were satisfied with the progress.

On Tuesday, Michael came to see him. They talked about the balance that Michael has to pay for the property, which amounted to six hundred thousand rupees. He already had in the bank at Quatre Bornes three hundred thousand rupees in his account and he may get a loan of three hundred thousand rupees from the same bank. There will be no problem to effect payment on the due date. "How far have you reached with the loan negotiation? Have you completed all formalities?"

"Yes, I think so. I am being helped by the branch manager and he said that he will submit my request to the headquarters for approval. Maybe the bank will request for a valuation of the property before disbursing the money."

"Anyway, there will be no problem on that score. Give the manager a copy of the title deed of Blackburn and tell him that this is the property that you will buy. In about fifteen days' time, you will be able to sign the contract and the property will be yours."

That evening, Dev was talking to Laxmi. She was in a good mood. They were in the television room. "We have a beautiful house and the strong cyclone could not cause any damage to it, except for the few window panes that were broken."

"Structurally, there can be no complaint but I think that the house can do with a coat of paint. What do you say?"

"It's a good idea to repaint the house and we should not delay in doing it."

"What colour would you prefer?" Dev asked.

"Let us start with the roof. We can have it in white. The exterior walls can be in cream with the edges in black. The rooms can be in light blue, light green, pink or some other light colour. The ceilings should be white throughout the house. Let there be a six-inch band in the corridors and in the rooms, of black colour. You can see what colour you would like for the kitchen."

"You have chosen the colours for the exterior, for the interior except for the kitchen. The kitchen is your domain and you leave only that to me. It does not matter. You know how beautiful some real antique furniture will look in our house. I do not mean second hand furniture, but real antique furniture."

"You tell me what is the difference between antique furniture and second hand furniture? To me it's all the same. People have used them and then they are tired of them so they sell them. Those who want to get a good price for them will never call them second hand but rather antiques, Those who do not care overmuch for the price they will get, or rather those who are honest, they will tell you that they are selling second hand furniture because they are buying new ones and they must make space the new ones. This is to me the difference between second hand furniture and your antiques. At the end of the day, they are all the same."

"They are not all the same. Antiques are antiques whereas second furniture is not even worth looking at. A mulatto is migrating to Australia. He is selling his old house. The house is not worth living in. Michael will buy the land and last time I accompanied him to have a look at the property. I know the man, he is called Edwin Blackburn. He has some furniture that he will sell to me. Even if you will pay, you will not get such furniture, and also they are made in solid wood. He has asked me to see him again, and if I am interested he can sell them to me but I can take the furniture only on the day he will be leaving the country. I will not put the furniture in the house, but in the spare room that we never use. I will have them varnished, then you will see if we can have them in the house."

On Wednesday, it was raining in the morning. Dev went to the shop around ten o'clock. Kader was waiting for him. Dev called him to the office. Kader said, "Mr Dev, I have got a copy of the plan and he asked me to have a look and if it is alright, he will submit it to the committee which will examine it and then the mayor will approve it. I do not think that I will need the approval of the CEB and the CWA because I know that my mother has just received the water bill. Maybe she will receive the electricity bill in a few days."

"Very good. Let us examine the plan," Dev said and he opened it on the table. He explained to Kader how the plan fitted his dream and if he will follow proper advice, he will make his mother a proud person. "Now get two or three copies of the plan made. But you cannot act until the plan is approved. Go and see my friend at the municipality and tell him that the plan is perfect; he can send it to the committee. Then you can go and do some work."

Dev went in the shop and he was satisfied that clients, especially tourists have started coming in again, as they used to do before the cyclone. He talked to one of his assistants. He asked him, "What would you say if we were to have some advertisement to promote the shop further?"

The assistant replied "We are doing well at the moment. Of course we have to, and can, increase our sale. On Monday, we shall be starting our first sale. I take it that we shall have a big crowd, and in the circumstances, we should recruit one or even two young persons to help us."

"Of course. We can recruit, for about two weeks, two young persons to help us. But I prefer to have somebody we know. My friend's maid was asking me to look for a temporary job, for about three weeks, for her son who is now on his holidays. They are poor people and the young man will use the money that he will get to buy his school effects. His father spends half of his monthly pay on drinks. You understand the type of man that he is. The boy is doing his last year at the secondary school. If you have somebody who will be interested to work for two weeks, get him or her, to come and see me tomorrow, if possible. Next month we must see if we shall need another full time employee. At the moment, two persons look after the shop, and one odd-job man and cleaner and messenger. Do we need another salesman? Think over this."

"Mr Dev, even if you recruit another person, don't you think that you should recruit a man and not a girl? According to me, it will be difficult to manage a girl in the shop. We shall talk about it later on."

Dev was thinking of the reason for which his employee was reluctant to work with a female staff. Dev then went in his office and started reading the Upanishad that he was reading the day before. He asked the messenger to get him something to eat. "Should I get some Dal Puris for you, Mr Dev? The Dal Puris of Maraz are very tasty, as you already know."

"Yes. Do that. And get me some tea also." And he continued reading the book.

At home, he told Laxmi, "We need a young man to work in the shop for two or three weeks, because we shall go on sale as from Monday next. I told you about this. When I was at the place of Ram, his maid was telling me that her son was looking for a job for two weeks to buy his school requirements. Why don't you talk to Maya and find out if the son is free."

"Let's go to their place this evening and we can talk to them."

And at eight thirty they went to the place of Ram. They explained about the temporary job and Maya phoned her maid. "Ruby, has your son got the temporary job that he was looking for…? Is he prepared to take a job in a shop in Port Louis…? Wait, Ruby. Maya said that Ruby said that the son was prepared to take the job but he could not go there by himself.

Dev said, "Tell her to come and meet me at our place at eight o'clock. The most important thing is that she should bring her son. I will explain everything to him." Maya conveyed the message to Ruby. They all chatted for about half an hour about politics and about the weather. And they indulged in some gossip.

The following day, Ruby brought her son before eight o'clock and she came early because she had to start her job at eight. And she left her son and went to her work. Dev told

Ruby's son what was expected of him. The boy grinned and agreed and Dev asked him how much he would ask for the three weeks work. The boy laughed and said. "Mr Dev, see yourself what you will give me. My mother told me to leave everything in your hands."

"Alright, but later on, don't say that I didn't pay you enough. Come on, let's go."

When they reached the shop, the assistant told Dev that he had brought his nephew and requested him to give him the job for two or three weeks, if possible. Dev told him to bring his nephew in the office. The assistant brought his nephew in the office, he called Ruby's son also and Dev asked all of them to take a seat. Dev asked Ruby's son's name. It was Kovilen. The assistant gave his nephew's name. It was Suraj. Dev asked him if he was at school. The young man said that he was doing his Higher School Certificate. Dev told the Assistant to explain to the two young men what was expected of them. Dev asked Suraj how much he was expecting for the three weeks' work. The boy said, "Give me whatever you like. I will be satisfied." The assistant was instructed to let them start their job right away, which was immediately.

Dev was reading the morning paper when his eyes caught the headline **"ATTACK ON THE PLANTERS BANK.** How much money was stolen when the Planters Bank was broken into? We have been informed that a total sum of sixty million rupees was stolen in that most daring robbery when the cyclone was hitting the country with a violence hardly ever experienced. The money has not been recovered yet. Who was the third person who allegedly was the brain behind the coup? It must be remembered that one person died in the course of the robbery, and the main culprit is unknown. He is supposed to have the booty. Where has all that money been stacked? We are talking of sixty million rupees.

"The bank does not want to give any further detail. It has only said that the doors have all been replaced, the electricity wires have been replaced and additional CCTV cameras have been installed.

"On a question put by us about some information on the identity of the master-mind of the robbery, the officer of the bank told us that this is evidence that be cannot disclosed now, because the enquiry might be prejudiced.

"When we contacted the Police, the Superintendent responsible told us that it is true that the third person is still missing and the money also has not been recovered. We shall be questioning further the accused who has been arrested, again to get some clue about the third person.

"On being asked when the enquiry will be completed, the Superintendent informed us that it will be difficult to close the case before the booty is recovered. On a question as to what will happen to the person who is on remand for the offence, how long he will be on remand, he said that soon the file would be sent to the Director of Public Prosecutions and we shall follow the directions that he will give.

"We have detailed one of our journalists to do some investigative work in this matter and we are surprised that the Police have made no progress to trace out the third man."

The Police are interested to solve crimes. For this purpose, the officers rely mostly on confessions by accused parties, and once the confession is obtained and recorded, the other pieces of evidence are brought in line with the statement of the accused party. And that is not a very difficult task.

How many cases are brought to Court that do not rely on confessions? This is a legitimate question. And how many confessions supposedly made by accused parties to Police Officers are challenged by the legal adviser of an accused party? And how many of those challenges are successful in the different Courts?

Why is it that Police cannot enquire into a criminal case, of whatever nature, relying on their own knowledge and training? That is they must discard any alleged confession, unless the confession is made before a Magistrate in Court?

Dev was thinking along those lines and especially about the bank robbery. He knows that the person arrested is innocent of the crime with which he is charged. How can he disclose this to the Police without putting himself in jeopardy?

He came to the conclusion that the person had the intention of robbing the bank, he had entered the building for that very purpose, but through no fault of his own, he was caught and his friend was shot dead. Can a person be convicted of having an intention to commit a crime? Or of an attempt to commit a crime, even if his attempt has been frustrated through no fault of his own?

Dev was sitting in his office but his mind was elsewhere. He heard something like a knock on a door, and the noise coming from afar, but then he realized that someone *was* knocking at his door. He answered and his assistant came in. Dev said, "You would not believe it, but I was feeling sleepy."

The assistant said, "Mr Dev, a man wants to talk to you."

"Who is he and what does he want?"

"He is one of the street vendors. He wants to buy all the articles that we are going to put on sale if we would give him all the articles with a discount of twenty five percent of the sale price."

"He seems to be an interesting person. Call him in, let us talk to him."

The man was brought in and Dev told him to sit down. The assistant was about to go, but Dev told him to sit down as well. The man gave his name, Irfan Gopal. He added that he had heard that the shop was putting its old stock on sale and he was interested in buying the whole lot at a discounted price of twenty five per cent less than the sale price. Dev told him that he has given his word to another street vendor and he does not want to be a traitor to that man.

Irfan said, "I know it must be Mael Boodhoo, or is it Ramjan Miya or Maan Baboo? Those people do not want to work in collaboration. We would then all be making a good profit."

"I am sorry that you have come too late."

"If I will reduce twenty five per cent of the discount to only fifteen per cent, would you consider selling to me?"

"My answer is still the same."

"I will make a last offer. Take it or leave it. I will buy everything on sale with a five per cent discount. I cannot go below that. What do you say?"

"My answer is still the same. I am sorry that I cannot satisfy you. If I will change my mind, I will contact you."

When Irfan had left, Dev told his assistant, "I would never like our articles to be exposed at a street corner and people saying that it is cheaper to buy from a street hawker than in the shop. I agree that the articles in the shop are a bit more expensive, but just a bit. However, our quality is better, we have a better service, plus we have an insurance cover."

The two new recruits were understudying the other assistant. They were told that they must learn by heart the pricing code, to be always polite to all the clients, however impolite they might be, because they must not forget that the clients are the kings.

16.......SATISFACTION COMES WITH HARD WORK

Dev was more or less back to his daily routine. He was always trying to help some people, at times going out of his way to do that, and he was satisfied with his life. When he next met Michael, he asked him how was his loan application at the Planters Bank proceeding? Michael told him that he had not heard from the Bank, he will go and talk to them.

Then Dev told him, "I have another plan of business for you. I have been thinking about it for the past two or three days. If you can think about a company which will recruit only people who have been pensioned off, this company will give those persons recruited some work according to their capacity and so a chance to earn some money, to meet friends and to keep themselves busy instead of doing nothing. I was thinking of people providing electrical services, plumbing services, painting of buildings, repairing and varnishing of furniture and servicing of motor vehicles.

"Say the company is divided into one hundred shares, you must have under your personal control, fifty one per cent of the shares at all times. A company is not meant to give jobs to relatives or friends. It must be run purely on business lines.

"The company will have a chairman, a managing director, a secretary and members of the Board. You must also have a treasurer. You must hold meetings, you must pay taxes if you make profits, you must ensure those working for the company and you must file regular returns. What do you say concerning this idea of having such a company?"

"Mr Dev, all this looks interesting but very complicated. How can I do what is to be done? What knowledge do I have in these matters? I have spent my whole life working for others."

"This is what I am telling you. You have worked for others. Now it is time to make others work for you. You start very small, you think of growing very slowly. You must not think of moving in a society that is not known or familiar to you. You must think that you are still working as you always have."

"I am afraid I will not be a success and fail you. Unless you would be part of the company."

Dev was in a quandary. He did not know what to say. He asked Michael to come to his place after six o'clock. We shall talk about the project.

Michael came as requested. Dev called Laxmi also. He started by putting a few questions to her. "Laxmi, quite often, you need the services of an electrician. What do you do then?"

"I ring up Michael and he comes and he does what he has to do. I have no problem."

"And what do you do when you need the services of a plumber, when a tap is leaking or you have a burst pipe?"

"Don't mention about plumbers. It is very difficult to get plumbers these days and the ones you get, most of the time, do not know much about their job. You must look for a good plumber for us."

"I am telling Michael that he must form a company. A group of people who are specialists in their fields will work for him. They will not be employed by him; they will work only when their services will be needed. They will not be employees who draw monthly or weekly wages. What do you think about this idea? Give your opinion freely and frankly. Don't you think that this is a good idea?"

Laxmi answered "The idea appears very praiseworthy, but who will look after the paper work and the finances?"

Before Dev could say anything, Michael jumped in, "Mrs Laxmi, I think Mr Dev can join me in the company as the chairman and adviser. Only then can the company move successfully. You must advise him to help me. He knows me well enough, since I first worked for you about thirty years ago. He can trust me."

"Of course we trust you, Michael, otherwise we would not have referred so many persons who needed the services of a good electrician."

They talked for some time and Michael left. Dev then told Laxmi that Michael had put him in a dilemma. He gave the idea of a company and Michael now wants him to be with him.

"I see no problem. You can help him. At the same time you can help others who would be needing the services that they would require. Furthermore, you would also be helping the people who are rather old in age but still hale and hearty. You should join him."

Dev decided that he would associate with Michael and form the company. The following day, he went to see his cousin the notary. He talked to him about the contract of sale of Michael. The notary asked him if he was in a hurry. Dev told him that the seller was going to Australia in a month's time, so the transaction had to be completed in a fortnight at latest. The purchaser is just waiting for the confirmation of a loan.

"I will prepare the deed of sale. What will be the price of the land?"

"He will buy only the bare land; there is an old building thereon, which is worth nothing. They have agreed at a price of six hundred thousand rupees. Isn't the price reasonable?"

The notary said, "I cannot say. It depends on so many factors. Anyway, when the deed will be registered, if the authorities would be of opinion that the sale price does not reflect the real price, the matter will be referred to the Valuation Tribunal and a fine might have to be paid."

"Prepare the deed which can be signed in about ten days. There is another matter that I would like to discuss with you. I have told Michael that he should start getting some people together; these persons should be expert electricians, plumbers, carpenters and mechanics. They would be persons who are retired and have been pensioned off, but still fit for the job they were doing before being pensioned off. They would not be employed by Michael, but they will be paid only if and when they will work. I have advised him to have a company for that purpose. I have come to see you to prepare the documents and incorporate the company."

"I will think about it and you can see me day after tomorrow. Tomorrow I am fully busy. Get the name of the company, and the persons who will be responsible for the various posts. I will see you day after tomorrow then. We are now finalizing a document for another client." Dev left the office and wanted to meet Dilip. He told the latter that the contract of the property should be ready soon and there would be the incorporation of a new company. He also wanted to know how much the fees and other expenses like registration duty would amount to, so that Michael would be ready. Dev got the answer and he went back to the shop.

Dev was satisfied that both Michael and Kader were by now fully interested in their respective projects. Michael would soon be the owner of a property, in spite of what people generally thought, that is that a Creole can rarely be a proprietor. But further, he would be controlling his own company. Kader would be the owner of a building – residential as well as commercial in which he could live with his mother and get married. Besides which he would be able to carry on his trade in all security.

On the following day, Michael saw Dev at the shop. He told him "I went to see the manager of the bank and he told me that he is prepared to give me the loan himself and he will charge the same rate of interest as the bank. He told me further that he will take a mortgage on the land I will be buying."

"We do not care who will lend the money, provided the interest they will claim will not be unconscionable. So you are ready to sign the contract?"

"As you say Mr Dev. Everything depends on you. See what is to be done, because the project is yours, I will simply follow you. I have already started talking to some persons who have been pensioned this year and they are interested to work in the company."

Next day was a Saturday. On the eve, Dev's assistant had requested him that it would be good to have him in the shop because they would be getting the sale procedure ready and the sale will start at nine o'clock sharp on Monday. He did go to The Shop. Everybody was busy in the shop, including the two part timers and Dev got busy, too. Some of the articles on sale were put in one part of the shop, but they all could not be accommodated in one place. However, the price tags were reserved to be affixed to the various articles after the shop was closed on the eve of the sale. Dev's assistant said "It's nearly time, Mr Dev, to close down. Do you want us to do anything further today?"

"No, not today. You will affix the price tags tomorrow at the last moment I suppose? I shall be leaving in five minutes because I have to attend a Teeluck Ceremony. I do not think that I will come down tomorrow, but I will see. Maybe I will come."

The ceremonies relevant to a Hindu marriage last for three days and they take place usually on Saturdays to Mondays. After the cyclone the wedding season, so to say, has again started and it will go on for some time. People will come to the shop to buy wedding presents and he should be prepared to make a good stock of such presents. He knows what the Hindus buy and he does not make a big profit on these items, he considers that he is doing his social service. Though the profit is not that big on individual items, yet on the number of items sold, the profit becomes good at the end of the day. Dev's shop has created a name for itself in presents of these types.

On Monday morning, Dev came to the shop at eight o'clock. Laxmi had come along with him. All the members of the staff were making the last arrangements. Laxmi was looking around and at nine o'clock sharp the assistant opened the shop to the public. About fifty persons had had been queuing up to get in first. Dev told Laxmi to be in the shop while he went to meet his cousin, the notary, to conclude the purchase of the piece of land that Michael was buying.

At ten o'clock, Dev went to the office of the notary accompanied by Michael. The notary called Dilip and asked him if the deed was being drafted and whether all the details are taken care of. Dilip asked how payment would be effected?

Dev said that it would be paid by cheque, the total amount. On the date of the signature of the contract, somebody will be lending Michael three hundred thousand rupees and Michael will bring a bank cheque for the sum of three hundred rupees. The person who will be lending the money wants to have a mortgage on the property."

"Another deed has to be drawn up for this other transaction and both contracts will be signed at the same moment. You agree Michael?" the Notary asked him.

Michael did not understand much of what was being said, but he said that he agreed. Dilip asked Michael to follow him because he wanted some details of the transactions.

When Dev returned to the shop, Laxmi was talking to one of her friends who had come to buy some gift items. Dev told them to go in the office which they did.

Dev asked the messenger to get them some cakes, some Dal Puris and some tea for three persons. In fifteen minutes, Dev went to have his lunch. Laxmi and her friend were still talking, but when they saw Dev in the office, the friend said that it was time for her to go. Dev told her to have some tea and some Dal Puris and Laxmi also insisted. So they all three ate Dal Puris and cakes and had tea. Laxmi's friend then left.

Laxmi told Dev that as they were in Port Louis they could go to visit their relatives in the region of Flacq. And they left the shop. When they arrived home around six o'clock, Kader was waiting for them in the street. Dev called him and he was introduced to Laxmi. "His name is Kader and we call him Long Kader. You remember I was telling you that his father was working for my dad and his mother was helping my mother. His house has been completely destroyed by the cyclone and he has nowhere to go. His mother is living with her sister, but for how long? He wants to build a house quickly, but he has to get all the permits. Thank God, government has decided that for such people, their files would go through a fast track procedure. His mother is a very nice person. She likes Indar a lot."

Kader told him that he had completed all the necessary procedures for the loan as well as for the permit of the house. He has to wait now.

Dev asked him if he thinks that the municipality will approve the permit of the plan as submitted? Kader said that according to the clerk it will be done.

Dev then said, "If it is so, why don't you get somebody to start digging the trenches to lay the foundation of your building? Of course you must get someone who will do the ground markings first, this is most important, because if the markings are not done according to the plan, there will be defects and faults in the structure."

The next day, Dev went to the shop early because he wanted to be in the shop during the sale time. He got the newspapers and there was a report in one of the newspapers about the bank robbery. That interested him immensely and the report said, "Our reporter who has been investigating the robbery has told us that the accused person could not have been one of the robbers because he has never been involved in any theft of such a magnitude. People do say that there is always a first time, but this man does not have the intelligence to participate in such a criminal activity.

"If there was a third man, it is surprising that the Police have not been able to trace that man yet. It is said that the third man was the mastermind behind the coup, and that man is supposed to have bolted away with the booty. We are told that sixty five million rupees have been stolen. And that the booty was made up of used bank notes. The question that must be asked is what would be the weight of sixty five million rupees? Can one person carry such a weight at one go, in the dark, vanish into the cyclonic weather after having told the two people who were with him to wait in the bank and that he would come for them after having deposited the notes somewhere upstairs?

"How did the robbers enter the strong room and then the vault? How much money does the bank keep in the vault? In the meantime, we are informed that the case file has already been sent to the office of the Director of Public Prosecutions. Would the accused person be judged as the sole perpetrator of such a big crime? Where have the sixty five million rupees vanished? It is to be remembered that the accused is on remand at the Central Prison, maybe waiting to be judged."

Dev was pondering over the matter, he was thinking of going to the authorities and telling the officers about the events as they really happened and the now accused would be released. But then he came to the conclusion that it will serve no useful purpose.

And then Dev also thought of the bank manager at Vacoas who was already rejoicing that he would have at a cheap price, in the end, the land that Michael would be buying. However, he did not know that he would be in for a big surprise.

What name to give to the company of Michael? He thought over it but could not come to a conclusion. At last he had an inspiration. "AT YOUR SERVICE CO. LTD". This is the name that he will propose to Michael.

The following week things started moving rather fast. First, Kader reported that he had had a prayer conducted by a Maulana at the site of the new house and then the trenches were being dug, and that the previous day, his plan was approved as expected. Dev gave him five hundred thousand rupees and told him to withdraw about fifty thousand rupees from the bank. He will use that money to buy building materials for the construction. But he advised Kader never to carry more money than was necessary. Kader bought a lorry load of sand, iron bars and cement and other materials, but just enough for the foundations. The mason told him to buy some wires, some nails and some second hand planks, which Kader purchased. The following day the mason came with an apprentice and started working. Kader went on his business for a few hours every day, and on his return he would help the mason. But he was under the impression that work was moving very slowly, and he could not do anything.

The following week, two officers of the Mauritius Housing Corporation called on Kader on the site. They had a look and told Kader he should not have started the building before they gave him the go ahead, but eventually informed him that the loan was approved but they would release it by instalments, depending on the stage of the construction. They informed him that he could see them at the MHC and he would have to sign some documents and the first instalment will be released.

Kader went to see Dev to inform him of the progress of work. Dev requested him to get a few more masons so that work could move faster, Kader told him that he must come and see and inspect what has been done so far. He insisted and Dev gave in. He promised that he would come at about eleven o'clock. Kader came to take him to the site and when he arrived, Kader's mother was waiting for him. She greeted him and said that she was happy to see him. She thanked him several times for doing what he was doing to help them. "Not even our relatives or family friends can do much for us," she said rather loudly.

For Michael also, things were moving satisfactorily. Dev went to Blackburn's place with him where Michael informed the seller that he was ready and they must tell the notary when Blackburn could accompany him to the office of the notary. A date was agreed upon. Then Dev talked about the furniture that would be purchased. Blackburn took him to see each item closely and at the end of the tour, Dev was told, "I will give them to you at a very reasonable price. Give me fifty thousand rupees and everything in the house would be yours."

Dev said his estimate is forty thousand rupees, and if it is agreed, he can pay him immediately. And he agreed to collect all the items on the day of their departure. Blackburn agreed and another matter was settled. On their way back, Dev told Michael that he could now n move ahead on his own. He could come to see him for the money. "I have done my duty," said Dev.

"Mr Dev, now it's not the time for you to abandon me. I shall be nowhere if you are not here to advise me. I would request you to be with me at all times. Please do not talk like this, my heart can fail."

Dev felt that he was trapped. He liked to help people, but he never thought that he will have to spoonfeed them. And he thought that now he had to help Michael to the end, and he had to be prepared for it.

Michael went to the office of the Notary with Mr and Mrs Blackburn and the notary explained the terms of the sale and other conditions that are relevant to such transactions. The notary said that, "Another document for the loan will have to be drawn up, which will mention the mortgage transaction. Both documents will be executed at the same time. Let me prepare the second document and we shall then fix a date for signature. I must get in touch with the lender to prepare the document." When Mr and Mrs Blackburn had left, Michael requested the notary to kindly ring up the banker at Vacoas, and he would give all the particulars that he needed for the preparation of the lending transaction. This was done. Soon the date for the execution of the documents was fixed and all the parties were so informed.

On the date when the deed was being signed, Dev removed another one hundred thousand rupees from his account to meet the costs of the registration dues and the fees of the notary. He handed it to Michael and they went to the notary's. The time for the signature of the documents was two o'clock. The notary read over the documents, the parties signed, two independent witnesses signed, and sale price was handed over to the notary. This was in the form of two office cheques. The notary said that the cheques were office cheques and so he had no problem paying the seller straight away with his own cheque, which he did.

"The documents will be sent to the Registration Office for transcription and registration purposes, this will take about one week." When Dev and Michael were alone with the notary, Dev asked him how much Michael has to pay for the registration duty as well as for his fees. The notary told him the amount and Michael paid him. He was told to collect the documents in a week's time.

Dev asked him about the formation of the company. The notary called Dilip and asked him how far he had got with the formation of the company. Dilip asked about the name of the company, the shareholding, the directors and other details. Dev said he would send all the particulars the following day, in the morning.

In the car, while they were going home, Dev told Michael, "I was thinking of a name for the company, 'AT YOUR SERVICE CO. LTD.' Or do you want to suggest another name?"

"I do not know anything about these matters. Do what is best for both of us."

Dev told him, "Let there be ten thousand shares of ten rupees each. You must always be the majority shareholder in the company, whatever may happen. Otherwise you may lose the control of the company and others will say that the company is theirs."

When Dev reached home, he asked Michael to get down as he would like to finish with the details of the company that Dilip had asked. They sat in the corridor and Laxmi served them two mugs of tea. Dev asked, "Who would be the chairman of the company?" Michael insisted that that post should be taken by Dev himself. Michael would be the managing director. And they thought of the other directors who could be trusted. When their work was over, Dev called Laxmi and told her what Michael had been doing during the day. She was a bit surprised but then said, "The idea of setting up a company is a good one. However, I am a bit skeptical about the transaction concerning the land. Will you be able to pay back the loan on time? Those people who lend money for such transactions are, most of them, sharks and crooks. You must be careful."

Michael said, "I think I can get the money to pay for the loan, Madam. I have my pension, I work hard even now and if the company will be successful, I can get some money from that also."

Dev handed him the document where he had written the particulars of the company and he said that he must leave it with Dilip and he must tell him to prepare the company deed as quickly as possible.

The following day, Kader came in the shop and informed Dev that everything was going on fine. He had started taking his business seriously, the building also was going on smoothly. The foundation was nearly complete and by next week, he could start with the walls. Dev advised him that, "You should not spend more than you can explain about sources of his finance. If the bank disburses one, you should not spend more than three of your own. Be very careful of relatives, of neighbours and friends. Never trust them because jealousy and hatred are the worst enemies you can come across. Now that you are building a house and a commercial complex, you will attract all manner of persons, persons who will become jealous of you, especially people you least doubted. So be on your guard. If the income tax authorities will come across you, be ready to answer them. Do not say that you earn very little nor so much that you must have paid income tax. You have worked hard; you have regularly saved part of your income. And you are constructing the building using your savings and a loan from the MHC. Do not forget these pieces of advice."

"I have to thank you for everything you have done for me. How can I forget your advice? My mother always talks about you and about Dr Indar and she says that I must not leave your doorstep. Two persons I am grateful to are my mother and you. In time, you will see if I am grateful or ungrateful." His eyes were full and he had to wipe them.

Dev asked him if he would need some money. He answered, "I will start buying the building materials."

"Would a hundred thousand rupees do?"

"Yes, Mr Dev. Thank you. In fifteen days, you can come and visit the site, you will be surprised."

"Whenever you need more money, do come. But be careful. You are not constructing all the floors now?"

"No, I will follow your advice. I will complete the ground floor, both the residential part as well as the commercial part. What do you say?"

"I would say how is the ground floor going? If you can make some savings on the loan of the MHC, you can just lay the blocks and complete the concrete roof of the first floor also. The refined works should be completed in about two years.

In about fifteen days, the company "AT YOUR SERVICE CO. LTD" was incorporated and it could start business. Mr and Mrs Blackburn left the country and they handed to Michael the keys to the house. The house belonged to Michael but the furniture and movables to Dev. Dev took what belonged to him and stored them in a big room in his house. That room was used as a store. Laxmi came to have a look at the second hand articles as she called, but did not say anything.

Dev advised Michael to ask for a loan, and in the meantime, he must have a building plan drawn up. "The person you should contact is somebody at the municipality working in the building department. He can draw the plan and he shall see that it is approved expeditiously. I will help you with your demarches. Go to the MHC, get the forms and we shall fill them in. Tell them that you are in a hurry, because you do not have a proper house to live in."

Dev was not satisfied with the manner in which the company 'AT YOUR SERVICE' was progressing. Not enough persons were contacting Michael for his services. Dev decided that the services should be publicized. Ten thousand pamphlets were printed and the distribution started at the fair of Vacoas where there is a huge crowd on Tuesdays, on Thursdays and on Saturdays. The recipients were told that they should keep the pamphlet in a safe place in case they would be in need of the services offered by the AT YOUR SERVICE company. The phone number and the services provided stood out; they were in bigger characters and in the colour red. The publicity had a positive effect and they were thinking of moving to rented quarters which were more spacious and people were impressed as the atmosphere was more business-like.

PART IV – CONCLUSION

17...ALL PERSONS ARE BUSY

Three months later, Dev was satisfied that both Kader and Michael were doing good progress. The concrete roof of the first floor of the building of Kader was laid. Every now and then the officers of the MHC were on the site to disburse further sums. He used to get a hundred thousand rupees every time he would be in need. He knows where to buy the building materials. He could afford to buy good quality materials, and this only the experts can tell.

In another three months, Kader and his mother were ready to move in the new house. Preparations had been going on for a week. He bought some second hand furniture and a few cheap new items. The much awaited day arrived. An Imam was invited to offer prayers. The chief guest was Dev and he came with Laxmi, as he was requested to do. They were received like royalty, to say the least. Kader's mother was never satisfied, she made Laxmi sit down in the best settee and served her some sherbet personally. And talked of so many things about the parents of Dev and the behavior of Dev and of Indar when they were young. Surprisingly, Indar also came a few minutes later. Kader told Dev that he had been to his place of consultation and told him that he must come. On seeing him, Kader's mother burst out crying and she held him tightly for some time.

Later they were served biryani. "It is chicken biryani. We have prepared only this because we have thought of you. You are our chief guest and you can be sure that I shall be sticking to a course of conduct that will always remind me of the help that you have extended to me. In every prayer I shall offer, I will ask for your welfare first. People can say what they want, I do not care," said Kader. Three artists performed for the benefit of the persons present. One was the singer, and he was the harmonium player as well, another was playing the tablas and the third person was playing the manjira, all three Indian instruments par excellence. The songs in Urdu and Hindi, were indeed beautifully rendered. Most were from Hindi films and some were Islamic religious songs and essentially in Urdu. Anyway, they had a good time and Dev and Laxmi felt obliged to stay till the last moment.

In the car, Laxmi told Dev "They consider us to be more than their relatives, as if a part of themselves. I find it very surprising especially that they had prepared that vegetarian dish for me. I wonder how they knew that I was a vegetarian?"

"When Kader came to invite me, I told him about this. I told him that you will not eat at their place. He told me that he will bring a vegetarian dish from the vegetarian restaurant that is found near the Cathedral. And this is what he did, I suppose."

About two months later Kader was ready to open his shop. He wanted Dev to come and see what arrangements he had made for the opening. There were two big rooms and each had a toilet in a corner. There was a wash basin and a place to eat. "I can rent one of the two rooms in case I get a client. What do you say?"

"It's a very good idea. But I would say open your store first and if you get some clients, other would-be tenants would be more interested in your building. The more clients you will get, the more interested others will be and you can then get a higher rent. What are you going to sell in your shop?"

"I will sell what I sell in the street, that is, I sell whatever I can buy from the manufacturers. Mostly I sell shirts, pants, dresses and such items. I have contacts among the managers of the big manufacturing concerns. Say one of the manufacturers has an order for the production of one hundred thousand shirts, he will not produce exactly one hundred thousand, he will produce five thousand more, to take care of the defects in some shirts, by defects I mean all types of defect, such shirts that will not be accepted by those who have given the order, for several reasons, when the order has been satisfied, what would the manufacturer do with the remaining shirts? He will sell them. He has already made his profit when the consignment has been accepted and dispatched. He has to sell what remains to people like us, the street hawkers. We get the shirts at a very cheap price and we can sell them at three times the cost price to us, or at times twice the cost price. That is why we insist on being street hawkers. We make a good living. Even if we are prevented by the Police to sell our goods in the street, we still persist to do so, and if we are taken to Court, which rarely happens, we are prepared to pay the fines that are imposed on us. We can afford to pay."

"But why is it that ninety per cent of the street hawkers come from one community only?"

"The reason is simple. You know that at one time, ninety percent of the community were the followers of one political party and the then Prime Minister from another political party said that the community will have to pay a price for having supported that particular party. In fact we were boycotted by the government of the day on all fronts. That was the time that we turned to become street hawkers, buying cheap and selling cheap, we attracted quite a number of clients with our way of doing business. We play one political party against another to continue plying our trade. The established traders have been complaining against us, they have been even to the Supreme Court, they have obtained a judgment against us, but who is going to execute the judgment? We are not against any political party, nor are we for any political party, for that matter. We are for those who, at the moment, allow us to do our business as we have been doing. But for how long can we go on like this? At times I think over this problem and I am glad that now I have a place where I will not be bothered by the authorities."

By then, they entered in the shop. There were counters, but no articles as yet. In the other room, there was a huge stack of shirts, shorts, trousers, dresses, jeans, underwear and what not. In one corner, was sitting the mother of Kader. She was busy examining shirts for defects. When she saw Dev, she rose from the table and kissed him on both cheeks and asked about news about Laxmi and Dev asked her if she was happy with her life. She said that that was what she was waiting for. She is very happy she said. And she added that it is time to get Kader married, to which Dev added, "You must look for a good girl, someone who can look after the shop and keep Kader in control."

Kader said, "During daytime, I am a street hawker, in the evenings, I work here. I verify each piece of garment, I mark the defects, and my mother repairs the defects. But the two of us cannot cope with all that we have to do. I must get one or two other persons to help us."

"I am glad to see that you are becoming a serious person. If you move in this direction. I am sure that in a few years' time, you will forget about your past."

"There will be an inauguration of the shop on Friday next. You will be the guest of honour and of course Mrs Laxmi also will be invited. It will be a very small affair, with about fifteen persons. I was thinking of inviting our Members of Parliament, but I cannot invite one only. The other two will feel frustrated. What is your advice?"

"My advice is that you are a businessman, keep away from politicians, do not let anybody know where your political sympathy lies. That will be the best course." They were going out when Kader told him, "Do you know who did the electrical wiring and installed the various apparatus in the building? Michael did it. He was responsible for all the electrical installations in the building. And a very good job he has done. I am grateful to you Mr Dev. I thank you from the bottom of my heart."

A few days after Dev had been to the place of Kader, this latter came to his place on a Sunday afternoon. The purpose was to invite Dev as well as Laxmi to officially open Kader's shop. He explained that the opening cannot take place except in their presence. He added that his mother has sent a special invitation to her. Both Dev and Laxmi said that they will be present. Kader then said "Not only your presence is necessary, but, Mr Dev, you will do the opening ceremony.

On the opening day, Dev and Laxmi arrived there at a quarter to nine. There were about twenty five people there. After a few minutes, Kader called everybody to the front of the shop to proceed to officially open the shop. Kader spoke for about three minutes and said how Dev had helped him and had it not been for Mr Dev, he would never have succeeded to have a house and, the more so not to have a shop. All thanks to him. "I shall forever be grateful to him," he concluded.

Dev was then requested to say a few words in his turn and then he was invited to cut the ribbon that was tied across the door of the shop. He did it and everybody clapped and then entered the shop. There were only garments in the shop, and the variety was rather limited. In time the shop will find its clients if Kader will have the will to spend time on it. Sherbet and tea as well as some Indian sweets were served to everybody present.

Dev was less busy in The Shop now that the sale period was over. The sale was a success and he felt that it should become an annual feature. He can then renew his stock a bit more often and have more clients. He was again thinking of recruiting another person to help the overworked employees. He did not put any notice of vacancy in the papers but told his contacts to suggest some names. They did suggest some names and eventually, Dev selected a middle-aged man. He was taken on probation of six months, and if he was found to be suitable, he would be confirmed. In fact the man started working hard, but his assistant reported that it seemed that he was a bit of a drunkard and if he would continue drinking, his services will have to be dispensed with.

Dev called him in his office. He told him, "I am not concerned with your private life. But in so far as you are working here, you cannot come to The Shop drunk. Everybody drinks. But they do not abuse their drinks. I am told that you were dismissed from your last employment because of a drink problem. What do you have to say?"

"Sir, I had a problem with alcoholic drinks but now I am trying to control it."

"You are married, you have a wife and three children and if you will not stop drinking, I am not going to employ you. Well, I would like to see you with your wife and three children here tomorrow morning. I would like to talk to all of you and then I will take a decision."

When Dev arrived home, he told Laxmi that she must accompany him to the shop the following day.

"Is there something very important that will take place in the shop? Otherwise you rarely invite me. Anyway, I will come. But at what time shall we be back? Because I will have to cook our dinner, besides, Renu will be coming home."

Dev just said that tomorrow will take care of itself.

On the following day, Dev arrived at the shop earlier than usual and Laxmi was with him. The shop assistant whom he had called to see him was already there. His wife and two of his children had accompanied him. Dev called them in the office. Laxmi was seated beside him. "So she is your wife and these are your two children. I have called you here to inform you that your husband, Madam, has the bad habit of drinking too much. That is his business; I will not get involved in such matters. But when he works for me, he cannot drink. And if he drinks, what effect would that have on his wife and children? Do you want to continue working here?" This last sentence was addressed to the shop assistant.

"I am sorry, sir. I would like to work here. I can tell you that I have thought deeply on what you told me yesterday. I agree to everything you say. I have realized how much suffering I have caused to my wife and children and to other members of the family."

"Why don't you join a Bhajan group or the Mandir nearest to your residence? You can go there once every week, early in the morning. Why don't you sit down and talk to your children and your wife?"

"I will try to do it. No one has ever given me such advice."

"I will suggest that for the next six months, on the understanding that you will work here, on pay day, your wife will come to collect your pay packet. So that you will not be tempted to go on a binge drinking. Would you agree to this suggestion? What do you say, Madam? I can give the necessary instructions to my assistant."

She started weeping. Her husband said that he would agree to this condition, provided she does not give part of his wages to her brother.

Dev asked the shop assistant to start work seriously. Dev also left the office telling Laxmi to talk to the woman to find out what was wrong with the family. She was to suggest remedial measures. Half an hour later, he came back to the office. She thanked Dev and Laxmi as well and they left.

Then Laxmi said that she had some shopping to do and she will come back before noon.

About fifteen minutes later, Michael came to talk to Dev. "Mr Dev, since moving to the new premises and the pamphlets that we have distributed, we have some more clients. I have bought a few mugs, some tea leaves, some sugar and some milk. I make tea for all those who work with us. Clients either ring us up or come to the office. They can always find a person to render some service to them and at a reasonable cost. And the artisans are very happy. I have told them the conditions under which they will be working, they have agreed. Now I am thinking of buying a table and a deck of cards and a box of dominoes. When they do not have anything to do, they can enjoy themselves playing some games. Every morning I buy a newspaper for them to read. They are very happy to see each other in the morning and when they finish their job they come back to the office to chat with each other and they like to laugh at the way in which they perform their duty. You must come and see them one of these days. They will feel that there are other people who can be trusted in the company."

Two or three days later, Dev did go to the office of "AT YOUR SERVICE CO. LTD". One person asked him if they could be of service to him. Another person said, "Don't you know him? He is one of our big Bosses." He then asked Dev whether he has come to see Mr Michael, and Dev said "Yes, I would like to talk to him." Michael was preparing tea and he brought a mug of tea for Dev as well. There was a bench and a few chairs and a table. They sat down around the table. Dev asked them if they were satisfied with the conditions of work. One person who appeared to be their spokesman answered for them all. He was the person who knew Dev. Dev said, "All the workers must be covered by an insurance policy in case they are wounded in their work. Michael, come to Port Louis one of these days and we shall see what is to be done. In case they have to go someone's residence, how do the artisans reach that place?" Dev asked Michael.

Michael answered, "Either they come to collect the artisan, or they provide some means of transport. Transportation is under the responsibility of the person for whom we work. They do not hesitate to pay for that." Dev then addressed to the workers. He thanked them, "for what you are doing, for the sense of service to the community as well as to yourselves. At the same time, you meet your friends and you can spend a happy time. You are not the employees of the "AT YOUR SERVICE CO. LTD", but rather you are here on the "work as work is available" concept. So there is no relationship between a boss and his employees. I really hope that the relationship between the company and people like you will last long."

18...HE IS SATISFIED WITH HELPING OTHERS

Dev was sitting in his office. He had called both Michael and Kader to his office. He had informed them that he had something important to tell them. When they arrived, he told them, "I called you here today to find out how you are doing. You know everything that has happened from the eve of the cyclone. You Kader, you have made a very good progress. You constructed your house, and by the way, it is a very beautiful house, and you have opened your shop. How is your business going?"

"It is quite slow at the moment. I am sure that it will pick up later on. People must know what we sell at what price. They will not get the articles that we sell at our shop at a cheaper price anywhere."

"You must advertise your shop. And how is your business as a street hawker going on?"

"That is going alright. Now that I have to look after two businesses, I am very busy."

"And what about you, Michael?"

"I have bought the land as you advised. I have asked for a loan from the Mauritius Housing Corporation to construct a building where there will be the residential part and the commercial part. It will be on the same pattern as the building of Kader. I will get the plan maybe next week. They are taking some time at the municipality. I must submit the plans for the loan to be processed."

"I am very happy with both of you. Continue moving right ahead and you will be satisfied with what you have done.

"Now there is another important matter that I must tell you. You, Kader, you have withdrawn from your account four million and five hundred thousand rupees. You Michael, you have withdrawn three million and five hundred thousand rupees. Do you agree?"

Kader and Michael looked at each other. They did not know what to say. After some time, Kader said "Mr Dev, you remember I told you that Michael did the electrical works at my place? He told me that he and you have formed a company and you are a minority shareholder. You can help me form a similar company and you will be the minority shareholder in that company as well. This will be my pleasure, sir, and I shall never forget you. Please do accept this request from me."

'"But what about the money? You must tell me if you agree with the account I have given you."

"Mr Dev, we have talked about this matter. You have as much claim over that money as we do. Whatever you say, we accept. We would like you to be a part of us."

"Kader, I will help you as I have helped Michael. I will be a minority shareholder in your company. But I am telling to both of you that whatever dividends will be paid to me would go to charitable institutions I will select. I also told you that I will not spend a cent of whatever money I have kept. I am true to my word."

The two friends left Dev's office. Dev was sitting in his office, musing about what had happened since the cyclone. He was neither happy nor sad; he had the feeling that he would complete his long cherished ambition when he would be ready to divulge what caused him to go against the Planters Bank.

He then started reading. These days he had been concentrating on religion, his religion, Hinduism. He was a follower of The Advaita philosophy of the religion. For a long time he was thinking of Death and what happens to the Atma, that is the Soul, when it leaves the body. And the book to read to have some ideas on the subject is the Katha Upanishad. Dev was a bundle of contradictions. He could be a very religious man at one moment and the next moment he would be promoting the idea of Nihilism. This made many of his friends say that Dev could discuss any topic, and from every side possible.

A month later, the mother of Kader called on Dev, and after greeting him, she said, "Kader has decided to get married. I know of a family in Phoenix, all the members are good people. They are not rich persons, they earn their livelihood honestly. The father is a messenger in the government school of the area and one of his sons is a nursing officer at the Candos Hospital. Another son sells vegetables at the Vacoas Market. They have three daughters. The first one is married, and the second one can be married to Kader. She is a very intelligent girl and she can help Kader in his shop. What is your opinion about the marriage?"

"I am very glad that Kader has decided to get married at last. It is high time that he settles down." At that moment, Kader walked in the office of Dev. His mother was surprised, and the surprise showed in her looks. So also was Dev, but to a lesser degree. He asked him to sit down. Kader asked his mother what she was doing in the office?

She retorted, "You think that you alone have the right to see Dev in his office? You think that I have no right to do that, is this what you mean? I came to see him—" She did not end the sentence she had begun.

Kader interrupted her, "See how she now talks to me, Mr Dev? As if I do not have the right to ask her why she has come to see you."

The mother said, "I have came to inform Dev that now you have decided to get married. We were talking about the girl and her family. I know that you will not say all that I can say."

At that moment, Dev felt that he could continue with the interrupted conversation. "I was saying that there is a right time to settle down. Kader, you should not miss the opportunity to marry when the right girl is chosen by your mother. I am very glad that now you think that you cannot carry on with your life as you have done."

Kader's mother said, "My sister, the one at whose place I stayed during the cyclone, it was she who talked to the girl's parents. You know they are all related. Now I have a problem. Kader told me that I should not talk about how he was living some time ago, but I think that sooner or later, they will come to know about it. This will bring a lot of criticism and as they are related to us as well, there is bound to be wide repercussions. I would not like that."

"I said that let us not talk about my past conduct right now, but wait for some time, that is, till after the wedding."

"Kader, I prefer to side with your mother in this matter. Would you like to be told that you cannot be trusted because you hid from them a vital piece of information? Vital not in so far as you are concerned, but vital in so far as your future in-laws are concerned. If they will not be interested to marry their daughter to you, let your mother look for another girl. She is bound to get a better girl for you. But I would say do not jump to any conclusion right now."

Kader's mother said, "Dev, I want to call the father and the mother to my place and tell them what to expect. I do not want to face my Creator with a guilty look. You must come as well. I will not call any other person except my sister. If they will accept the marriage proposal, we shall fix a date for the wedding, if not, another person who lives in Glen Park has informed me that his relative is looking for a young man for his daughter. I want to settle the wedding very quickly. Can you make it this coming Sunday? Of course you must come with Laxmi, we would like to have her opinion as well. Besides we like to see her and talk to her. We expect you to come at about two o'clock."

Kader said, "Ma, you haven't asked me whether I am free on Sunday at two o'clock. And you haven't invited me. I will not come." This remark made them smile.

"Kader, you must be serious when we talk of serious matters. You cannot take everything so lightly. You must grow up and take your responsibility."

"Mr Dev, I came to tell you about the plans of my mother to get me married, but when I came here, I saw that my mother has overtaken me. So we shall see you on Sunday."

On Sunday, Dev and Laxmi arrived at the place of Kader. The mother of Kader was talking to three persons. At the same time Kader entered in the room. His mother introduced Dev and Laxmi to the other persons. "This is Mr Dev and his wife, Laxmi. They are more than relatives to us. They have always helped up us in everything we do. You have heard of my son Kader, but you had not seen him before. And Dev of course you have not met my sister here. She is related to Mr and Mrs Carim Hossen. They are the parents of the girl we were talking about."

They then started to indulge on some small talk. Kader's mother and his aunt went in the kitchen and brought sherbet for everybody. Then Mr Hossen said "Mrs Reekye, you wanted to talk to us about the relationship that we are trying to establish between our two families. I think that we are ready to listen to what you intend to tell us."

"Yes, Mr Hossen. I consider that nothing must be hidden when we are trying to build a relationship. My sister here has been the intermediary between our two families. You do not know my son, so I have decided to give you his background.

"My husband was working as a driver with the father of Mr Dev and I was working as a maid in their house. The relationship that we developed was very strong. When Kader was still small, my husband passed away. My husband had a piece of land with a house thereon, made of timber and iron sheets. My sister lives two houses away. She used to help me, I was working and a widow came to stay with us. She gave us a small rent.

"All told, we had no problem for food, clothing and a shelter. But we did not have money for other things. I did not have to beg for anything. Kader had his primary school education but he could not go to college. He started to learn work in a mechanic's workshop. But he did not stay there for more than three years, though I told him that he could have a good life as a mechanic with his workshop in this place we are now sitting in.

"But that was not in Kader's destiny. He started doing some odd jobs, wherever he could get the chance. He then fell in the company of some bad persons. They exploited him to the maximum. In the end, he was caught by the Police and the Court sent him to Prison because he was made to accept that he was the only person to have committed the offences. Before that, he had appeared before the Court two or three times and at that time the Magistrate had fined him on each occasion. But I can tell you that at heart my son is a very good man. He does not have a criminal streak in him. Since he went to prison, he has learnt his lesson that there is nothing to replace hard work and sincerity. A relationship is cultivated on sincerity and if there is no sincerity, the relationship will not last long. My time to meet my Creator is approaching fast. I would not want to be told, even when I am gone, that I have hidden something important from you.

"This is what I had to tell you and I called you here. Do you want to say something, Dev?"

"You have said everything that needs to be said. Perhaps I can add something. My family has been resident of Port Louis. After my marriage I moved to Vacoas and I lost track of Kader who could have been around eight at that moment. And I did not meet his mother either. I again met Kader after over twenty years. The meeting was a stroke of luck. I was going somewhere in Port Louis and somebody approached me. He identified himself as Kader, and my memories came floating back to me. He was a street hawker, he told me. His mother had this piece of land. The cyclone blew down the house standing on it. He had no choice but to get a loan, build his house and a commercial section as well. Now he has started a shop. If he will take his work seriously, he will be a very successful person."

Mr and Mrs Hossen had listened to Kader's mother and to Dev in silence. Eventually, Mr Hossen said, "I have listened carefully to what we have been told. We appreciate very much that you do not hide anything from us. But may request you to give us two or three days to think over what you have said and we shall return back to you?"

Three days later, Kader came to inform Dev that, "Mr Hossen has rang up to say that they accept to marry their daughter to me."

Dev was happy with this piece of news. He told him so. Then he added, "Kader, is there a school, either a private or a government school, primary or secondary, near your house? The reason I am asking you this is because you can consider opening a small place where you can sells cakes, sweets, some Dal Puris, and what children appreciate."

"This is a marvellous idea Mr Dev. I know how to attract children. There is a secondary school nearby, and most of the children go through the shop. And there is a factory a little further up, where you have men and women working in day as well as night shifts. I wonder why this idea did not come to my mind."

"Then you must have a separation in the shop, a section where you intend selling the snacks and cakes and other edible things and the shop proper. There is enough space for that I suppose."

"Yes, sir, there is. I can free a space of about three metres wide right through to the end, that is about ten metres."

"Create an enclosed space of three metres by four metres. There is no need to have a door in front, but there must be a door in the rear, that will allow access. In the front, there will be an open window bay of about two metres, through which you will be selling your cakes and Dal Puris."

"Thank you, Mr Dev. I am going to work on the scheme and you will hear about this in a week's time. He started going away, but then he said, "I am sorry I forgot to tell the main reason for which my mother sent me to you. She said that the marriage will take place in about two months' time; you and Mrs Laxmi must be fully involved in the whole process. What should I tell her?"

"Tell her not to bother."

He went home and was having some tea and talking to Laxmi. There was a phone call. It was from Michael. He wanted to see Dev and was asking if he could. "Yes Michael, you can come immediately."

"Michael wants to see me. Now he rings me up before coming. Anyway, that is a good initiative."

"Previously, he was not the manager of a company. But be careful that he will not be deceived with your ideas. He is the manager of a company, what will happen if he cannot pay his employees? You have asked him to take a loan to buy a piece of land. Now you have asked him to take a loan to construct a building. He does not have any experience to enter into that kind of business. That's why I am telling you to be careful."

By then Michael arrived and they went to sit in the corridor, their usual meeting place. Michael started, "Mr Dev, I got the plan of the building from the employee on Monday last. At the MHC, the officer who has my file told me that they will expedite to process the loan. You remember you filled in the form for one million rupees."

"Yes, and now you must clear your land of the rubbles. You haven't received any notification from the Registration office that the value of the land is much more than the declared value? If you have not received such a notice, take a few photographs of the property from all angles, especially highlighting the bushy parts and the other outgrowth, to show that the property was in an abandoned state. The house must appear that it was an abandoned structure and it has to be removed. After that you can remove the building, sell it or demolish it then sell what can be sold. When the land is cleared, you must put in place boundary stones…"

"Mr Dev, how can I fix boundary stones? I do not know anything about this. I am scared when I hear such matters."

"I can talk to Dilip, he can help you. I will ask him to call on the site. You prepare five or six iron pegs about a foot long and get a hammer to fix the pegs."

"I will do that."

"When you have completed clearing the land, you must start digging the trenches to lay the foundation."

"I will get somebody to mark the area of the building and trace the trenches."

"Now tell me about the company. Is it progressing satisfactorily?"

"It is going on alright. We have more clients than when we started. Every day, we receive about ten calls, these calls require the services of electricians, plumbers and a few say they need the services of the mechanics. We received a call to repair some furniture but I can say that we are progressing slowly. We are not making losses."

"Now you must remember that we are operating a company. We must abide by the legal provisions of the country. We have to inform the Registrar of Companies about certain matters. Then we have to file Income Tax returns. You must have a secretary to do that, a part time secretary, someone who was working in the Income Tax Office. He can come once a week and I shall talk to him. He can be the accountant as well. You are keeping a book concerning all the income the company receives as well as all the expenses that are incurred."

"This I am doing Mr Dev. That is why I told you that the company is not making any losses. We are as they say, not in the red."

"It's a question of time, you will get used to what you should do in different circumstances. I shall come and have a look as to what you have been doing. I can do it more often, but then you will not learn the job of managing your company."

"My wife knows about the company. She has asked me to thank you for everything you have been doing for us. And my useless son-in-law wants to be part of the business. My wife was telling me that I can employ him. My daughter also has been pestering me. I have said no, it cannot be done."

"If he wants to work on the same conditions as the other workers, and he does not ask for any favours you can give him some work. But never treat him as a member of the family when he is working, but strictly as somebody who is working in the company. If he accepts these conditions, then give him some work, whenever there is any of course."

"This is what I had to inform and discuss with you. Thank you, Mr Dev."

"Michael, before you leave. I need the services of a cabinet maker to varnish and put right the furniture I bought from The Blackburns. Can I have such a person?"

"We have a cabinet maker in our team. He is already taken up tomorrow. I will send him to you day after tomorrow."

"But you must treat me like any other client of the company. This will show the workers that there is no preference for the directors of the company. This will show our seriousness in business."

When Michael had left, Dev talked to Laxmi about the cabinet maker. He told her that he will be working for about a week. "Then you will see which item of furniture you are going to keep and the rest we can give to some needy person."

The following day, arrangements with Dilip for fixing the boundary stones of the property of Michael were made. Then Dev went back to reading his book on Religion and Spirituality.

When Laxmi arrived from her shopping, Dev asked the messenger to get some Dal Puris and some cakes, together with some tea. They ate and Dev said, "Let us go to see some relatives today. Let us go to Curepipe where we can meet your Aunt and Uncle. Your cousin the doctor will be here in a week and he might get the impression that we rarely visit your Aunt when this is not the case.

19......WHAT CAUSES A PERSON TO CHANGE HIS OUTLOOK GENERALLY?

Three months later, the business of Kader was going on very well. His Dal Puris and cakes and other sweets had found favour with the school children as well as with the factory workers. He was not preparing them at his place, but he bought them wholesale from somebody who was supplying to the sellers in the central market. His garment business also was progressing but very slowly.

A tenant had come to have a look at the other part of Kader's building because he wanted to take it on rent to start a restaurant. There was not enough space for cooking and washing the dishes. "If I can have a part of your residence for that purpose, we can come to a good agreement," he said.

Kader went to see Dev and explained to him his predicament and Dev suggested that it would be better for him to complete the first floor of the building as quickly as possible. Dev gave him another five hundred thousand rupees and Kader got busy with the work.

He did not have enough time to devote to his business as a hawker, therefore he employed somebody to do that for him, so that he would not lose his place in the street and his friends would still recognize him as one of the first hawkers. His wedding was fixed for the following week. Laxmi told Dev that it would be a good idea if they could go the Kader's place and find out if everything for the wedding was being well taken care of. They did go and the mother of Kader told them "Thank you for coming and for taking an interest. Everything is under control. People of the Jamaat are helping us. You can come here whenever you want, it is your house. But you must take some responsibility on the wedding day."

The wedding was being held in a hall and the ladies were assembled in another hall, and the two halls were within walking distance from each other. There was not the usual crowd that are seen at a typical wedding. Dev was called to take part as one of the relatives and several persons wondered who this stranger was. However, Dev could not say anything, he simply did what he was told to do. The ceremony itself was not a long affair and soon people in the hall started moving from the hall. Dev had to be with the groom, they first went to the place of the bride and then to the place of the groom.

A week later, Dev and Laxmi were invited to a dinner at Kader's. There were only five other persons, the father and the mother of the bride, her elder brother, the aunt of Kader and her son. Kader had to explain what was the relationship of Kader's family with Dev and how far in time it went.

Dev felt that he had done what he wanted for Kader and now he felt free. But he had to invite Kader and his wife and his mother for dinner, and he invited them for a Sunday. The mother of Kader was surprised and she did not want to go, saying that she has never gone to a dinner that sounded a bit official. Eventually, she relented and all three went to Dev's place at seven o'clock. They had their dinner and Dev and Kader sat in the corridor for a chat.

"You are satisfied with everything that has happened concerning your marriage?"

"Yes, Mr Dev. The first floor of the house will be ready for occupation in about one month then we shall be shifting from the ground floor. The ground floor will be used for commercial purposes."

"Now that you have someone to help you in your business, you must find out what your wife would like to do. I am sure she would like to take some responsibility. You can give her the responsibility of either the snack area or the shop.

Your mother will have the responsibility for the other. But you must see to it that there is no conflict between your wife and your mother. You will not be able to take sides with your mother against your wife nor sides with your wife against your mother. The situation must never be allowed to reach that stage."

"This is the last piece of advice I am giving you. Except to add that you must have a part time secretary for the company, and that person must look after the income tax matters also. A retired officer can help you.

"Then you have some money with me. I would like to hand it to you, and I will feel really liberated. I know you will not forget me. But you can manage now."

"Mr Dev, please do not talk like that to me. I am what I am because of you, without you, I shall cease to exist. Please do me the favour of not using such a language." And he started weeping, quietly at first, and then he began sobbing rather loudly. Laxmi came to see what was happening and Dev said that nothing was the matter, but she was to see to it that the others should not know that there is something wrong. After a quarter of an hour, they went inside where the ladies were sitting. Kader addressed his wife, "Razia, you do not know the persons at whose place we have dined today. Believe me, they are the best persons you will ever meet. If you have any problem in life, knock on their door and you will be able to get some relief. I really mean what I am saying. They are more than my relatives and most important of all, I am proud to say that if I am here it is because of Mr Dev. I would like you to remember this always. You will come to understand both of them after some time. I thank them from the bottom of my heart. Mr Dev, Mrs Laxmi, please accept our thanks."

Michael got the boundary markers fixed and started buying the materials for the construction. He bought them in small quantities, just to complete the foundation. Before he started laying the foundation, he waited for the inspectors of the MHC to visit the site. In fact they came and told him to come to the MHC to collect the first instalment of the loan. He had six masons, all friends of his and they worked hard. In one month, the walls of the ground floor were early completed. They were ready to cast the first concrete roof.

Michael used part of his own money and part of the loan from the MHC. Because he was paying his mason friends well, he was getting a first class service. The inspectors of the MHC also were satisfied with the rate of progress. The disbursement of the loan was being made at regular intervals. In six months, the building was ready for occupation. Dev advised that Michael should lease part of the building to the company, and it took some time to explain that the company is a different legal personal from Michael's personal business. He understood at last and had a contract drawn up and the secretary signed for the tenant and Michael signed as landlord. He found it funny that he was leasing the building to himself.

When the first floor of the building was furnished, Michael moved to the new apartment. He made his daughter and his son-in-law understand that he had no place for them in the new house. If they wanted to, they could look for a new place of their own where they could live in peace. Or they could stay in the cite where Michael had spent his entire life. There were some problems with his wife as well as with his elder daughter. The daughter did not want to stay away from her mother; the mother wanted the son-in-law to be with them. Michael put his opinion forward. He said that a son-in-law cannot depend on the father-in-law. It's time that he started getting a job that can feed his wife and himself. He definitely did not want to have someone depending on him to feed him. He said that he could give him a job, but he would have to accept the same conditions as the other workers. If there is work, he will be paid the same rate as the other workers. However, he has no place in his house, and this applies to his wife, that is Michael's daughter, as well.

He added, "I think that I am clear enough. Now I am asking both of you, would you stay in this house or are you going to move out and look for other accommodation?" His daughter started weeping, this did not change Michael's attitude, eventually the son-in-law said that he will accept to live in the house in the cite. Michael then continued, "And I don't want you coming to my house scrounging for food every other day. You live your life and let me live mine in peace and harmony.

"You remember that I was not for your marriage with your husband. I still remember what you told me then. I have not forgotten that till now and this memory will last all my life."

Michael had definitely become a member of the middle class, with all the prejudice that this brings in its wake. But he was getting more serious in life. He was not working for other people, but others were working for him. He felt like a boss, but this entailed a lot of change in his life. He was not as carefree as in the past. His relationship with his former colleagues also changed. He was now moving with a different group of people. He was living outside the cite, and he felt like a different person.

Both Kader and Michael were now leading different lives from what they were used to and they had changed into different people now. Where would they have been had they not been helped by Dev? Were they better off? In terms of pecuniary benefits, definitely. In terms of social changes, maybe yes, or maybe no. Only time will tell. Dev felt that he had done what he thought to be the best for two persons who could not have lifted themselves from the condition in which they were stuck. Both persons did not have the will nor the capacity to get out of the economic and social rut in which they found themselves. Dev was not interested in deriving any pecuniary benefit from the business of either of his protégés; he became part of the respective companies that were set up on behalf of them. After a few years, he prevailed upon them that he must withdraw from their companies, but he assured them that he was always with them for any help they might need. On this condition, they agreed.

In two or three years, he gave them the rest of their money that he had kept in the shop, and that was the last attachment that he had with either Kader or Michael. Both Kader and Michael told him that he should keep what money they had with him for his personal use, but Dev told them that he goes by the original agreement. He has not used the money of the bank for his personal use and later on everybody would know why he did what he did.

He started thinking of the past.

He remembered the day on which he had told Laxmi that he was going to a religious retreat for a week and in fact he joined a group of persons who were the devotees of a Swami. They were taken to a secluded place in a building situated on top of a hill. All the persons were taught Yoga, Prayers in Sanskrit and the Swami translated the prayers in English. They were further given lessons in the philosophical aspect of Hinduism. They were given an idea of the various books and other authorities on Hinduism. At the end of the retreat, Dev felt that he had not had enough, he would have preferred to stay a few days more, but the retreat was for seven days and not more. Dev learned a lot on Religion, but he learnt more to reason out for himself. He thought that he was after all, an ordinary human being with all the faults and good qualities that such a person normally has.

Again he thought about what he did during the cyclone, and whether it could it be justified on moral grounds. He knows that legally, his action could never justified, there was every reason to take him to Court. But then looked at from another perspective, what is Justice? When the bank, or the officers of the bank robbed him of what was lawfully due to him, he could not get Justice. Could he fight a system that would not give him justice? What was he supposed to do in the circumstances?

After all, the Courts will apply the laws that are on the statute books. But statutes are passed by human beings, human beings with all their faults and foibles, human beings intelligent or not intelligent at all. But morally, he was right, though in the eyes of the law he was reprehensible.

And then there are officers who conduct enquiries. How far can they be trusted that they act fairly in their job? What happened to the person who was caught in the bank? He was innocent yet he had been sentenced to imprisonment for a long time. Is this justice?

20…..TRAGEDY STRIKES AT THE INOPPORTUNE MOMENT

Twelve years down the road. The shop of Dev is still doing well. He does not want to extend it because he does not have the place for extension. His employees have aged not only in terms of age but also physically. But they are happy at the treatment their boss gives them. The last employee to join the shop, the one who had a liking for the bottle is now one if the best employees, though his pay is still collected by his wife.

And then tragedy struck. Laxmi was not keeping in good health for about a week. A doctor came to see her, and the doctor diagnosed some sort of a viral fever and he prescribed her some medicines. The doctor assured Dev that there was nothing seriously wrong. Dev told Laxmi that he would go to The Shop and he would come back in a couple of hours. When he was in The Shop, there was a phone call to the effect that Laxmi is very ill and that she was asking for him. The call was from Laxmi's sister Renu. Her voice had a sound of urgency and Dev understood that he had to rush home as quickly as possible.

Telling his assistant that he had to go home as maybe there was some problem, he left without saying anything further. He could not think coherently, and he drove his car instinctively. There were two or three cars parked in the street near his house. One of the cars belonged to Sunil. As soon as Dev stopped his car, Sunil opened the door and Dev got out and walked inside the house. Laxmi was in the bed, her sister and the maid Neela, were quietly shedding their tears. Dev then came to know the bitter truth. Laxmi was no more.

Dev sat down on the bed, he held the hand of Laxmi and could not say anything. He just kept looking at her, as if he had lost the power of speech. How could anybody make him talk? That was the problem. Other relatives came, but he was not conscious of them. He could not care for anybody; he was concerned with the fate of his wife that was all that mattered.

Dev was thinking about his marriage that had been held more than fifty years ago, he could not say how those fifty years had passed so quickly. It appeared as if the wedding took place but yesterday, but he wondered how would he live on his own? It was not possible for him to exist without Laxmi; that was the conclusion that he arrived at.

More parents and friends arrived soon. Some close relatives started to take the furniture from the sitting room to other rooms, to the corridor and even outside. A few lady relatives took Laxmi for the ritual bath after two or three male relatives had taken Dev in the sitting room. A sofa was placed for him to sit. Next to the sofa were placed a few planks on the floor. On the planks were placed some grass usually called Kuss, and on the grass was placed a new piece of white cloth and the last resting place in the house was ready to welcome Laxmi. Sometime later, she was brought in the sitting room. She was dressed in her best sari, sindoor was put in the parting on her head. Dev was told to apply the sindoor which he did mechanically.

Other relatives started reading from the scriptures, from the Ramayana and singing religious songs. By nine o'clock, there was a huge crowd at the place of Dev. They all came to meet Dev, for a minute or less. Then they went out. A tent had been put up in the yard and plastic chairs, about five hundred, had been placed in the tent and people could sit down. People kept coming and going and this kept on till around three in the morning of the next day. Everybody expressed surprise that Laxmi had gone without giving any sign of the imminent departure. During all this time, Dev just sat near the lifeless body of Laxmi. He did not move, he did not talk and he spent the whole night in this position. Everybody who came had a few words for him, but how could he respond? What could he say? He was not feeling like crying nor getting up from where he was sitting. He thought how is it that he is sitting with Laxmi for the last time in life?

The mind of Dev went to what he had read on Hinduism; especially to a book which he had not yet completed reading. He remembered the title *The Mystery of Death.* It was one of the Upanishads, The Katha Upanishad, of course the original is in Sanskrit, but as most of the other persons, he relied on English translations.

The book is very interesting and especially for those who want to know what death is, the more so as all Hindus believe that the Atma, the Soul, is indestructible. So what dies? Where does the Soul go when it leaves the body?

In the morning, other persons started coming. Politicians of the different political parties came; the Prime Minister was there as well as some of the Ministers and Members of Parliament. The Prime Minister sat with Dev for quite a long time and kept talking. They were used to each other for such a long time. Of course there were the neighbours and especially the friends of Dev and Laxmi. Many people were saying what a good person Laxmi was, always ready to help, even at the cost of her own comfort.

The cremation was fixed for two o'clock in the cremation grounds of the family, where his father as well as his mother were cremated. Dev was thinking that his turn will soon arrive, sooner than many people expected.

The time for the prayers would soon start, before proceeding to the cremation ground. The priest arrived. The son of Dev was detailed to set the fire to the pyre, some relevant prayers for the occasion was recited by the priest. The body was brought outside. A bier was brought. It was made of bamboo and covered with leaves and flowers. The body of Laxmi was placed therein and the bier was placed in a van. Women were crying loudly, many men were quietly sobbing. The whole procedure was so sad to witness. Many persons accompanied the funeral procession to the cremation ground.

Dev rode in the van, so did his son. When they arrived at the cremation ground, there was another ceremony and five close relatives of Dev participated therein. They walked round the pyre seven times. The cremation pyre was already built by persons who work in the plantation of Dev. They had used only branches of a mango tree and the branches of another tree giving a nice perfume, the cypress.

The pyre was set on fire by the son and there was a raging fire soon. What and where is life when the body is consumed by fire in about two hours? Dev and his son returned home in Sunil's car. The priest also came and both father and son were told what they should do in the coming days. The son who had set fire to the pyre was given a stick after prayers had been recited. An earthen lamp was lighted where the body of Laxmi rested for the last time. The son was requested to stay indoors for three days and he was supposed to sleep on a mat for the three days. The lamp was everyday brought near the outside door so that at the end of three days, it is taken out. There were other ceremonies for ten days, for fourteen days and then there was to be a ceremony at the end of the first year.

Dev was feeling lost without his wife. He had never thought that he was so dependent on Laxmi for everything, be it for their home, for The Shop, for developing his relationships, for taking care of relatives, for discussing any idea, in short for everything. And yet, she was so quiet. How is it possible for him to do so many things by himself, alone? When Laxmi was alive, he just accepted her presence without saying anything. He never complimented her, though he was the first to find faults with her. Laxmi never took that so seriously.

That night Dev was sleeping alone in their big bed. He could not forget the mannerism of Laxmi, her way of speaking and how she was speaking to Neela and to other persons. He barely slept in spite of his having stayed without closing his eyes for two days. He kept thinking how he could depend so much on his wife when he had always thought that he did not need to rely on anybody for any service but on himself.

The following morning, he woke up early and he had to look for his clothes by himself. He did not know where in the closet his clothes were kept. At that moment Neela arrived and she gave him his clothes without any comment. After his shower, Dev was given tea without milk as was the custom in the particular circumstances. The priest came again around ten o'clock. Dev, the son and the priest went to the place of cremation and they looked for some pieces of bones and some ash, collected them in an earthen jar and took them to a place called Tamarin for the purpose immersing them in the place where the river meets the sea. This completed, they returned home. What home? Dev kept thinking. How could a home exist for him without Laxmi?

That night Dev went to bed early. After some time his tears started flowing, and it went on and on, he was then crying and he could not stop. Eventually, he fell asleep, when he woke up, it was already eight o'clock. Sunil came to see him and they talked about the arrangements he had made about managing the household matters.

Dev told him, "Neela has offered to look after the house and the household duties. There will be no problem on that. Another person, a man whom I have known at the Ashram will be coming in the evenings, all seven days of the week and the maid who usually comes for washing and ironing the clothes, would come on Saturdays and Sundays. The real problem is that I am feeling very lonely, and that is very difficult to accept.

"When Laxmi was here, I took her for granted. She did everything for me, but I did not then realise that she was taking all those responsibilities. I could not ever think that there was so much work to do. It would have been far better for me to have gone and for Laxmi to have stayed behind. You know Sunil, reading high philosophy in the books, discussing about life and death with learned persons is completely different from experiencing the death of a person near and dear to you. You know that sooner or later, you too will have to go, but is anyone ever prepared to go?

"Anyway, tomorrow I will go to The Shop for a few hours. I must try to keep myself busy, not physically, but mentally. And this is more difficult."

"Come home tonight, you can have dinner with us, we can have a chat and you will not feel so lonely."

"Not today Sunil. After dinner, you can come here for a chat." So it was decided.

Dev did go to The Shop. He did not say anything to any of his employees. He went straight to his office. His assistant immediately came to see him. "Mr Dev, I offer you my condolences. It has been a sudden blow that came without warning. Please do not hesitate to tell us what needs to be done, we are all here to do it. I am not talking about The Shop only, everything that needs to be done at your place, just tell us. What I know is that the mystery of God cannot ever be known to us, however learned we can be."

"I thank you, I know how concerned you are about me, and I shall not hesitate to call upon anyone of you in case I shall need your services."

One by one, the other employees came to offer their condolences and they all appeared to be affected by the tragedy of Dev. At one o'clock, he was ready to leave for home. He did not have anything to do at home, but he did not want to stay in The Shop either. But then, Kader came to see him. He looked at Dev, his eyes filled with tears, and neither could speak for a few moments. Kader sat down in an easy chair and then spoke. "You know that you just have to tell me what is to be done and I will do it."

"I know, Kader. How is your business going? Is there any marked progress?"

"Yes, Mr Dev. My son and my daughter are at school, my other son is at home; my wife is in charge of the snack. I can tell you that she is doing better than the restaurant in the other part of the building. My mother now stays at home; she rarely goes to the shop. I look after the shop. I now have three employees but I have to keep a close eye on them. You know how it is with employees."

"The restaurant people still occupy the residential part of the building for restaurant purposes as well as the commercial part?"

"Yes, they have extended the restaurant. We must say that they serve good food and the price is very reasonable compared to some other restaurants. And I am happy with them as tenants. Mr Dev, come with me to have a look at my business and to sit down for five minutes. We will all be so happy."

"Not now. I shall do it next week."

Dev went to the place of Michael where he found Michael rather busy. He just asked one of the persons working in the office to look after the business. He took Dev to see what he had done. There was a place in the building where the wife was preparing and selling snacks and cakes. She expressed her condolences to Dev and told him that they are always present to help him. They went upstairs and sat down in the lounge.

Michael told him, "My-first-son in law is working in the company. But he is not getting any preferential treatment. He is a worker as any other. I have allowed him to stay in the house in the cite; that is the only favour I have done to him. He has now understood that I mean business. His wife helps her mother. The second daughter also helps her mother. She stays in Rose Hill, with her-in-laws. You know, her husband is a Police Officer.

"What can we do to ease your pain a bit? I can understand how difficult it must be for you to be without your wife. I saw how devoted she was to you and nothing and nobody can replace her. Only time can bring some solace, but time takes too long for that. Anyway, I am always here for you, as well as my family. Mr Dev, where and when can I find someone like you?" And his eyes became moist.

Neela was preparing his dinner when he arrived home. Neela gave him a mug of tea, just as Laxmi would have done. Dev had given her a key to the house so that she could come and go at any time. Around five o'clock, the other person came. He did some odd jobs in the house and at six o'clock, he served Dev his dinner. Dev ate very little; he did not feel like eating. The man left and then Sunil and Renu came. They stayed till ten o'clock. When Dev was all alone, he felt uneasy, as if he was missing what he valued most in life. He put the television on, but it was difficult to watch. He had to switch it off. He closed the door and went out walking in the nearby streets. He returned home around one o'clock at night and tried to get some sleep.

The next day, Dev did not go to The Shop. He had tea and went into his office. He got a writing pad and started writing. He kept on till Neela came to see him. "Mr Dev, are you well? Because you have not come out since this morning and I was getting worried. I have prepared some lunch for you and if you are ready to eat, I can serve you now."

Dev replied "I do not want to eat much Neela. Serve me just a little bit, say half of what I used to eat."

After lunch, Dev went back into his office and continued writing. Around three o'clock, Neela served him tea, around four o'clock, he called it a day. Now he started feeling a bit normal, not totally though. That night he could manage to sleep rather well.

When next he was in The Shop, he asked his assistant how was the business progressing? The assistant brought the sales book and it was obvious that it was doing well. He had a look at the cash book, at the journal and at the ledger. A clerk in one of the ministries came in the afternoon, twice weekly, to write up all the books. Dev was satisfied.

Again Dev went home early. He went in the office and he got busy with his writing. At six o'clock, the worker told him that his dinner was served. He went to have his dinner and came back again to his writing. And he wrote till two in the morning.

Next day, Renu telephoned Dev and asked him to come and have dinner with them. When the helper came at five o'clock, Dev told him that he would not be having any dinner and he could leave as soon as he had finished doing what he had to do. He left at half past six.

Dev went to the place of Sunil, they had a nice chat, and thereafter they had dinner. Dev arrived home at eleven o'clock and went to bed directly. In the morning, he collected some documents from his office. He went to The Shop and from there he went to see his cousin the notary.

He said, "I have five envelopes in this big envelop. And I would like you to make a will for me."

"Why are you in a hurry? You have plenty of time to do that. Next week I am going to India for a month. I would be going alone. Don't you want to join me? I will go to Banaras to do some Puja. Come along, this will take your mind off from the difficult moment that you have had to endure."

"I was about to tell you that I will ask Laxmi and let you know but now I realize that this cannot be, ever. I can do the necessary Puja in the name of Laxmi and Banaras is the right place for that. In fact, I have kept some of her ashes for that very purpose. On what day are you going to India?"

"I am leaving next Friday in the evening. On Friday I will be working in the office and I will be leaving home around six o'clock. Do you want me to talk to my travel agent?"

"On one condition. My will must be ready before then. If you can complete with my will then you can talk to your travel agent."

The notary called Dilip and gave him certain instructions. Dev took out from his pocket a sheet of paper on which he had written his instructions for the will. The notary took the sheet of paper and read it. The instructions were clear and not complicated. "Would you bring your witnesses or should I get colleagues of mine to witness your will? Would you accept this?" He asked Dev.

"Get your colleagues as witnesses."

"It will be ready on Monday, at eleven o'clock we can sign it." He gave the sheet of paper containing the instructions to Dilip and told him to prepare a draft of the will. He then rang up his travel agent and asked him to reserve another seat for his cousin who would travel with him to India. Dev took the telephone and gave the details to the agent.

The notary further asked him "What about the big envelope? What do you want me to do with it?"

"This envelope is most important to me. When I will be dead, open this big envelope and give the five envelopes inside to the persons to whom they are addressed. I am not at liberty to disclose what has been written on the documents in the envelopes. You must take this matter very seriously."

"Alright. You sign on all the sealed parts of the envelope. Then I too will sign." Afterwards, he wrote something on the envelope and made an entry in a book used for the purpose. He opened his safe and put the envelope in. "It is in safekeeping here and your instructions will be followed to the letter."

In the evening Sunil and Renu came to see Dev. "Next Friday, I shall be going to India to perform the ritual Puja for Laxmi at Banaras. My cousin the notary is going to the same place and he asked me to accompany him. I could not have thought that I would have such a chance."

Renu said "We also would have liked to come for the Puja, but time is too short for us to get ready."

"If there is anything to do or look after, do let us know," Sunil said.

"There is nothing specific. You can just come and have a look at the house every now and then. If there is anything amiss, Neela will inform you."

On Friday Dev was gone to India in the company of his cousin. All the ceremonies were performed in the first three days. Then the two went visiting the hinterland and finally landed in Calcutta. They stayed there for another week and soon it was time to return home. And they arrived on a Sunday.

Dev could not get Laxmi out of his system. He had the feeling that she was around all the time. He missed her too much. How can there be so much attachment between two persons who did not know each other till they got married? How to define such a relationship? Is there a rational explanation for this type of bond between two persons? Dev thought and thought but could not get any answer.

The next day, he went to The Shop and met all his employees and talked to them one by one. He called Kader and told him that he would visit him the following week. Then he went to see his cousin the notary and talked to him about his will and the letter that he had left with him.

When he arrived home, he told Neela that she should not tire herself unduly and that she should take some rest every day. Then in the evening he paid a visit to Sunil and they talked for two hours. Renu told him to have something to eat, but he politely refused. At about ten in the night, he returned home. He went to bed. When Neela came for her duties the next morning, she opened the door and went in the kitchen. She prepared Dev's usual breakfast and waited for him to come for his breakfast. She did not hear any noise which usually came from the bedroom or the bathroom and it was so quiet as if there was nobody at home. Neela thought that maybe her boss had gone out early in the morning, but she had some sort of foreboding that something was about to happen or had happened. She went near the bedroom and called "Mr Dev, it is time to get up. Mr Dev, do wake up please, it is getting late. She opened the bedroom door and had a look in the bedroom and saw Dev in bed, as if in deep sleep. She called him again but there was no response. She immediately called Dev's son who lived in a house standing on its own but in the same compound. He arrived immediately.

The death of Dev could only be noted and certified. The son called Sunil immediately, he came and relatives and friends were called. Many of them did not want to believe that Dev was no more. The family doctor said that he suffered from a massive heart stroke and he passed away in a matter of minutes.

Dev's daughter was at that time on holidays in London She was called and immediately, she made arrangements to come home. She could catch the same day flight.

In the afternoon so many relatives, friends and neighbours came, and also a number of politicians. Dev's cousin the notary was there. The Prime Minister came and he stayed till quite late. When the notary saw the Prime Minister, he went to greet him because their respective families were well known to each other.

It was decided that the cremation will take place on the following day at around ten o'clock. By then it was expected that Dev's daughter would have arrived. A tent was erected in the yard, chairs were brought and people started coming. Dev was given his last bath, he was dressed in white and was laid on a new carpet on which was spread the Kuss grass and covered with a length of white cloth. An earthen lamp was lit near his head. He was covered with another piece of white cloth and relatives and friends started reciting prayers, religious songs were being sung and verses from the Ramayana were being read. The Ramayana is the book par excellence for the Hindus, and it is used on different occasions when the relevant verses are read and explained. Every family has some members who are proficient in that and their services are required on a regular basis.

The daughter arrived from London around eight o'clock. At half past nine, the priest came and Dev's son was to light the funeral pyre. He got ready for the ceremony and prayers were recited. And the funeral proceeded to the cremation place where Laxmi's mortal remains were cremated barely two months previously. Dev's body was laid on the pyre and it was covered with pieces of wood. The funeral pyre was set on fire and soon the remains of Dev were but ashes.

Was that the end of Dev? Obviously no. His history could not end so suddenly and people were expecting much more from him. Many people were really sorry to miss his company. He was the one person who was ready to give a helping hand in all circumstances. And even to strangers. But two persons were heart-broken. The first one was Long Kader, who came to the funeral with his wife and his mother. And the second one was Michael who came with his wife and two daughters. Both these men were sobbing and people did not understand why they were behaving in this manner. Nobody could tell them of the reason, not even those two persons concerned.

Two days after the cremation, the Notary opened the big envelope that Dev had entrusted to him. There were five smaller envelopes in it. The first one was addressed to the

Prime Minister. The second one jointly to his two children. The third one to the Chairman of the Board of Directors of the Planters Bank. The fourth one to the Director of Public Prosecutions. And the fifth one to the Commissioner of Police.

There was also a sheet of paper which contained certain instructions on how the notary should deliver the envelopes.

The Prime Minister should be sent his envelope by special delivery. Two days later, the notary rang up the office of the Prime Minister. He told a secretary who he was and informed her the purpose of the call, he just had to deliver a message. He had to tell her what the message was. The secretary told him that she would get back to him if he would leave his phone number. Half an hour later, the secretary rang him up and the notary could speak to the Prime Minister. He told him the circumstances in which Dev had instructed him to deliver the envelope.

The notary forwarded the envelope immediately to the Prime Minister. The Prime Minister received the envelope and instructed that he should not be disturbed. He then opened the envelope and read the contents.

21...THE REASON FOR WHICH A FIXED SUM OF MONEY WAS WITHDRAWN FROM THE BANK

"Dear Mr Prime Minister,

"My maternal uncle Chandresh Laljee was a bachelor and he was a very hard worker. He had his plantation, his transport company and he owned shares in various companies. About ten years ago, he decided to sell all his assets and he deposited the proceeds in the Planters Bank. He stopped all his business activities and was living off the interest that his affairs generated. He started travelling to different countries.

"When he was seventy five years old, he decided that it was time to retire completely and he became religious-minded. He told me that he is going to make a will and he will leave all his assets to me. Of course he did not have any liabilities. A week before he passed away, he called me at his place and reiterated that he had seventeen million rupees in his bank account at the Planters Bank and that I must be careful how I was going to use that money. That was the last I saw him alive.

"When he passed away, his will was read and with the necessary documents I went to the bank. There I was well-received and one of the higher officers informed me that there was a sum of two million rupees which they could transfer to my bank in my name. I was somewhat surprised that only a sum of two million was in my late uncle's account when barely a week before he passed away, he had informed me that there was a sum of seventeen million rupees in that account.

"I went to the Bank again and I told the officer who I had met the last time to verify the account again because it appeared that there was some error in the computation. I explained what I considered to be the error but I was assured that my uncle had withdrawn fifteen million rupees in three instalments a few days before he passed away. I was shown the withdrawal documents and everything appeared to be above board. I consulted a legal advisor and he accompanied me to the Police headquarters, in the office of the CID. I gave a declaration; the Police took down my statement and started an enquiry. I was eventually informed that there was no case as all the documents appeared to be genuine and had not been tampered with. The legal advisor advised me that it would be unwise to spend money as there was no credible evidence to start a case in the court.

"I did not give up because I was sure that my uncle had not withdrawn fifteen million rupees as I was persistently informed. Eventually, I withdrew the two million from my late uncle's account. One of the CID officers had told me that there were five or six cases where the heirs of persons who had passed away in the past two years had found their accounts depleted. Outside his hours of duty, the officer helped me with information on those cases. I contacted the heirs concerned and I was assured that the deceased in each case could not, and did not, withdraw substantial sums from their accounts a few days or a few weeks before they passed away.

"I was not expecting to get real and hard evidence that the account of my uncle had been tampered with. But I was sure that fifteen million rupees had been missing from his account and the Bank was responsible in one way or another. Legally I could not do anything to recover that money, but there must be some way to get what is lawfully mine. So I prepared a plan.

"I bought a commercial building not far from the Planters Bank. I refurbished it and opened The Shop, which, by the way, thank God is doing very well. I had to wait for three years when the conditions became favourable for me to put my plan in action. I had waited for three long years for a strong cyclone to hit Mauritius. When cyclone Mady was approaching our country, I thought that would be the occasion and if I missed that opportunity, God would not give me a second one.

"I could not do this thing that I had planned on my own. I contacted two persons I had known and associated them with my plan. They just followed me and I led them throughout. On the day when the cyclone was at its strongest, when no one was venturing outside, not the watchmen nor the police officers nor the people supposed to save the lives of those who were about to lose theirs, I took my two associates to the Bank. When a peal of thunder sent a deafening noise as if to help me, I blew the front door of the bank.

"We went inside, surprised the watchmen and used chloroform to make them unconscious before tying them up. I removed fifty million rupees from the vault of the Bank, not a cent more, nor a cent less. When we were coming out of the Bank, we untied the watchmen and escaped to our hideout.

"Later on, I learned that three persons had broken into the Bank, one of whom was killed, the second one was captured and the supposed third person had vanished with sixty million rupees.

"When we came out of the Bank we saw two persons coming on the street. We merged in the wall of the Bank expecting that we would not be seen. It was very dark but the two persons had some sort of light with them. They came near the main door and saw that the door was damaged. They went inside the Bank and we then continued on our way. There never was a third person. The dead man and his companion were not accompanied by a third man. And I am quite sure that they did not rob the Bank. How the Police Officers conducted the enquiry in this case is not known to me. I am told that once a person who is arrested makes a confession the authorities are satisfied. The person who has made the confession is prosecuted before the relevant Court, is found guilty and he is given the punishment that suits the crime.

"What happened in this case? Did the person arrested make a voluntary confession or was he induced to make the confession by unfair means or for some unknown reason?

"The question that has to be answered is this: why did I remove fifty million rupees when I had the opportunity to remove much more? There was a reason for this. I lost fifteen million rupees due to the negligence or the fault of the Bank. The Bank should have ensured that the money was in safe custody and it was their fiduciary duty to do so. This they failed to do. Therefore they must make good to me the fifteen million rupees. They also owe me interest as well as a sum for the damages that I suffered. I consider that a sum of five million rupees would be a reasonable sum for the interest and damages. So the sum of twenty million rupees is taken care of.

"We are left with the sum of thirty million rupees. Right from the beginning, I had pledged my word that I will not spend the thirty million rupees. You must understand I did not appropriate the money of the Bank, the twenty million rupees I gave to two deserving persons and even from that sum, I did not take a cent or derive any benefit therefrom, either directly or indirectly.

"Now we are left with the thirty million rupees out of the fifty million rupees. That sum I have kept in a safe place and the Bank can collect it at any time. The reason I retained this sum is simply to point out that the Bank must be very careful with other people's money. That sum of money is in a hidden safe in the Shop. It is hidden behind the wooden paneling in the wall of The Shop's office, and which can be accessed by opening a wooden paneling door. The help of the Police would facilitate the process.

"Over and above the sum of fifty million rupees that could not be accounted for, but which now can, is a matter for the Bank itself to explain. Who are the persons who have defrauded the Bank and misappropriated such an unknown sum? I am quite sure that an enquiry by people outside the Bank can give the beginning of a solution to the whole problem of theft from the accounts of the Bank's clients. This letter is copied not to the Chief Executive Officer of the Bank but to the Chairman of the Board of Directors, and the reason for doing so is obvious.

"The last point on which I am laying some emphasis is the manner in which the enquiry was conducted by the police in the alleged case. The man who has been convicted in this case was, in my view, innocent and he has been wrongly convicted. Shouldn't he be released from Prison immediately and awarded adequate damages for wrongful imprisonment?

"If anybody thinks of judging me, he should judge the Bank first, and it will then be clear who is the guilty party.

"Mr. Prime Minister, I have just given you the facts concerning the supposed theft and matters related thereto and part of my opinion. If based on these facts and on the opinion expressed, you can appoint a committee to enquire into the matter, you will help in uncovering the truth in these sordid affairs. And people will be grateful to you.

"Yours sincerely

Dev C.N

Copy to -

1. The Chairman of the Board of Director of the Planters Bank

2. The Governor of the Bank of Mauritius

3. The Director of Public Prosecutions

4. The Commissioner of Police

22…ACTION TAKEN

The Prime Minister read the letter three times. He kept thinking about what he would do. He asked his secretary to get the Governor of the Bank of Mauritius, the Director of Public Prosecutions and the Commissioner of Police to his office the next day for a meeting. She phoned them up immediately.

The notary rang up the son of Dev and requested him to call at his office. The son who was a government employee asked him if he could come immediately and on the Notary saying, "Of course, you do not have to have an appointment to see me." He arrived in fifteen minutes and the notary gave him the envelope addressed to the two children. "If you have any problem, never hesitate to contact me, otherwise what is the use of having relatives?" Dev's son said, "Yes uncle, I will do that. After all, you are one of the elders in the family and I will have to rely on you now."

The notary told him "Next week we shall read the will of your father. You and your sister must be here. I will let you know the date and time in due course."

The son did not want to open the envelope in the absence of his sister. So he kept it in his brief case. The notary sent the envelopes addressed to the other persons by his messenger.

The Chairman of the Planters Bank called for a special meeting of the Board and after considering carefully the letter, decided to have an enquiry conducted by experts outside the Bank. "There will be no interference in the enquiry and I want to know where the truth lies. After all, if there is even an iota of truth in what the letter reflects, we must know how the

Bank is being managed henceforth. Do not try to protect anybody, those who do so will have to answer for their conduct. Gentlemen, the reputation of the bank is at stake." There was no discussion on the matter, everybody agreed with the Chairman.

The Commissioner of Police read the letter, called for his deputy, showed him the letter and asked for his opinion. He said that there must be a meeting of the top officers to decide on the next move. So the meeting was called. The officers decided to call for the officer who was responsible for the enquiry in the bank robbery case. He came and said that the accused person voluntarily made a complete confession. The Commissioner told him there would be an inquiry into how the enquiry was conducted, there is other evidence pointing to other persons who had removed the money. So you be prepared answer some awkward questions.

The Director of Public Prosecutions read the letter. A file was opened and the letter was sent to the officer next in rank in the office of DPP.

Everybody concerned with the meeting with the Prime Minister arrived a few minutes ahead of time. They were sitting in the waiting room when the Prime Minister's secretary told them that they could go in the office. The PM did not waste time in preliminaries, he went directly to the subject matter he wanted to discuss.

"The purpose of this meeting is to find out whether what is contained in this letter has any truth. Each of you has got a copy of the letter and now I want to know what happened in this case. Now Commissioner, what is your comment on this letter?"

"Sir I received the letter only three hours ago. I must discuss it with my assistants then we shall take the measures that would be appropriate.

The Prime Minister got angry, very angry. People will have to pay for their incompetence. Nobody interrupted him. He asked the Governor of the Central Bank "What is your opinion concerning the allegations in the letter?"

"My opinion is that there may be some truth in the allegation. I think so because quite a number of similar cases have been reported but police enquiries have not disclosed any evidence of any criminal offence having been committed in all the cases. But we cannot go only by what the police have found or rather, not found."

"Who can conduct such an enquiry? I do not trust the police, or rather I do not trust most of the officers in such enquiries."

"I can call for a team working in the financial fraud section of the World Bank. Those working in the team are completely independent, but they will need inputs from our police. They are from different countries, very capable and real professionals in their field.

The PM turned to the DPP, "Would there be any legal problem as we shall be looking into the private affairs of the Bank?"

The DPP answered, "I do not think so, Prime Minister. All the cases concern fraud and they are criminal cases and they can be enquired into by the authorities."

In the end it was decided that two enquiries would be set up. First, there would be an inquiry presided over by a Judge into the case of the Bank robbery and whether the enquiry was conducted in accordance with the accepted procedures; the terms would include a suggestion of remedial measures in case there was some fault on the part of the enquiring officers.

Secondly, The Governor was instructed to start the ball rolling to get the team from the World Bank and let them work in collaboration with our police officers. Two matters were insisted upon. The World Bank people would not be working under the police force, but the police officers would be working for and with them. Let the police officers who would be detailed for the job be detached from the force temporarily.

When the children of Dev met that evening, they decided to open the envelope. In it there was a copy of the letter addressed to the Prime Minister and another letter addressed to both of them. The son read the letter addressed to them,

"My dear children,

"By the time you will read this letter, I will be no longer with you. I would have gone to meet your mother. You can now read the letter addressed to the Prime Minister and you will understand what I have done. Did I commit a criminal offence? I do not think so.

"However, whatever your conclusion, do not judge me too harshly. I could not go against the wishes of my beloved uncle.

"Sometime in the coming days, the testament will be read and you will understand that I have always wanted your progress in everything you do and please, be on good terms with each other. Life is too short for petty quarrels to affect you. I will always be everywhere with and for you.

"Your father who adores you,

"Dev C.N.

"P.S You may now read the letter addressed to the Prime Minister."

Both brother and sister read both letters and they could not help weeping like they had never done before. They were thinking of their mother and their father as they were feeling so lonely.

In due course, the will was read and both children were instructed how they should partition the property that had belonged to their parents. They were further instructed not to divide the Shop. They should set up a company in which they will each own forty per cent of the shares and the remaining twenty per cent to be distributed among the employees. One of them may take over the management of the shop and the other will be his assistant. Dev added that in all circumstances, they should be honest in their dealings and above all, they should be honest and true to themselves.

That is the end of the history of Dev. How would you judge him? Not too harshly I suppose, as he himself said: He was a human being after all.

EPILOGUE

The Prime Minister held a press conference to inform the people that the government had decided to institute a Committee to enquire into the case of the breaking and entering in the Planters Bank in all its various aspects, more especially in the manner in which the police conducted its enquiries.

Furthermore, the governor of the Bank of Mauritius decided to have an enquiry conducted in several cases where there had been complaints of fiddling in certain accounts of clients.

The Press had reported lengthily on the events. Speculation was rife and slowly, news started percolating that Dev was behind the two enquiries. The news was getting persistent and one of the papers published the letter that Dev had written to the Prime Minister. This created an uproar and overnight Dev became the hero of the lower and middle classes. Everybody talked of him and most people said that they knew him as an upright person who was always ready to help anybody who needed his services.

The biggest compliment came from those who said that Dev was a real man, he could take a Bank of the calibre of the Planters Bank and at the same time the police force in his stride. These two organisations are supposed to be sacred cows, no one dares to face them head-on, but Dev did it. Talks were held in his name, banners were floated and there were some processions all in the name of Dev.

People were following the works of the two committees through the papers and the radio and television. In about three months, the first committee gave its report. The enquiry conducted by the police was bungled and the alleged confession of the accused party was obtained by fraudulent means, through unfair means and through violence and promises exercised by a person in authority.

Three police officers were immediately suspended from duty and it was advised that they should be prosecuted.

The person who had been found guilty of the offence and sentenced for twenty years imprisonment was recommended to be released and a substantial compensation be awarded to him.

People were delighted, there were rejoicings everywhere. Only a week after the first committee gave its report, the second committee's report was out. This committee also came to the conclusion that there was a group of five officers of the Bank, most of them from the upper hierarchy, who had used fraudulent manoeuvres to drain the accounts of persons about to die thus depriving the heirs of what should have gone to them. The five officers were suspended from duty and they were to be prosecuted.

People went wild with excitement. The Bank recuperated its thirty million rupees but immediately, the Chairman of the Bank made a declaration.

"We are thankful to Mr Dev for having taken the trouble to enquire into his own case and the result has been convincing. He has rendered us an immense service. He was thoroughly honest and the Bank is grateful to him.

"We shall not take back the thirty million rupees that he so securely kept on behalf of the Bank, and which we have brought to the Bank. We are going to request the University of Mauritius to create a Chair using the thirty million rupees. And we are prepared to give a sum of twenty million rupees as damages to the heirs of Mr Dev."

Four months after his passing away, a friend of Dev wrote an obituary which was published in the newspaper the *Mauritius Times*.

"Dev passed away three months ago. He was a friend of everybody and an enemy of nobody. He was born in a family of professionals and grew up among books which he possessed by the thousand. He went to the best schools, he went overseas for his university studies, but, given that he had an independent mind, he did not stay long at the university.

"He went to the Soviet Union and to the countries in the Soviet Bloc. He moved from country to country helping certain International Organisations in translation duties, he was very proficient in both the English and French languages. His services were appreciated by all.

"Lately he became the owner of The Shop which has been a successful venture. That shop was a meeting place of Dev's friends, and friends he did not lack.

"He lost a sum of fifteen million rupees because of the corruption of the Bank wherein this sum of money was kept on deposit. He could not get justice through the legal avenue, but he did justice to himself, and by what means! I do not think that anybody will have the courage that he had; it takes a real man to do what he did. His relatives should be proud of him. What he did will live in the memory of the country for a long time."

A friend of Dev and proud to say so.

Shiv Ramessur. 21.12.02

THE END